# I WISH...

## THE WISHING TREE SERIES, BOOK 2

## AMANDA PROWSE

# CONTENTS

# PRAISE FOR AMANDA PROWSE

'Amanda Prowse is the queen of family drama' –
Daily Mail
'A deeply emotional, unputdownable read' – Red
'Heartbreaking and heartwarming in equal measure' –
The Lady
'Amanda Prowse is the queen of heartbreak fiction' –
The Mail Online
'Captivating, heartbreaking and superbly written' –
Closer
'Uplifting and positive but you may still need a box of
tissues' – Cosmopolitan
'You'll fall in love with this' – Cosmopolitan
'Powerful and emotional drama that packs a real
punch' – Heat
'Warmly accessible but subtle . . . moving and inspiring'
– Daily Mail
'Magical' – Now

www.amandaprowse.com
**Facebook:** https://www.facebook.com/amandaprowsepage
**Twitter:** @MrsAmandaProwse
**Instagram:** @mrsamandaprowse

Published in the United Kingdom by Lionhead Media
ISBN 978-1-915400-00-0 (paperback)
ASIN B09BJYK3VN (eBook)
FIRST EDITION
Cover by Elizabeth Mackey Graphic Design
Printed in the European Union

*For our wonderful readers in My Book Friends*

ALSO BY AMANDA PROWSE

**NOVELS**

Poppy Day

What Have I Done?

Clover's Child

A Little Love

Will You Remember Me?

Christmas for One

A Mother's Story

Perfect Daughter

The Second Chance Café

Three and a Half Heartbeats

Another Love

My Husband's Wife

I Won't Be Home for Christmas

The Food of Love

The Idea of You

The Art of Hiding

Anna

Theo

How to Fall in Love Again; Kitty's Story

The Coordinates of Loss

The Girl in the Corner

The Things I Know

The Light in the Hallway

The Day She Came Back

An Ordinary Life

Waiting To Begin

To Love and be Loved

**NOVELLAS**

The Game

Something Quite Beautiful

A Christmas Wish

Ten Pound Ticket

Imogen's Baby

Miss Potterton's Birthday Tea

Mr Portobello's Morning Paper

**COMPILATION OF ALL SEVEN NOVELLAS**

Something Quite Beautiful

**MEMOIR**

The Boy Between: A Mother and Son's Journey From a
World Gone Grey (with Josiah Hartley)

**CHILDREN'S STORYBOOK**

The Smile that went a Mile

# CHAPTER 1

'*L*inden Falls ten miles.' Sophie bounced in the passenger seat and read aloud from the sign as their roomy hire car, a 4x4, coasted along the wide, sweeping road with an abundance of trees on either side. The sky was cobalt blue and bright. The sun, high in the sky, filtered through the leaves to make dappled patterns revealing stars of daylight through the canopy above them.

'It feels remote.' Verity felt a flash of nerves as they drew closer.

'It's a bit different to London!'

'Just a bit.' Verity kept her eyes on the road, still not quite used to driving on the wrong side of the road and the fact that the steering wheel was where the passenger usually sat. Once or twice on the drive from Burlington International Airport, she had momentarily gasped, glancing across at Sophie to see her hands were not on the nonexistent wheel, this and the fact that her girl had not passed her driving test. She was also glad of the diversion of driving, worried that without it, her daughter might see the naked fear in her eyes.

It had felt exciting and daring in the planning; even the packing for a three-month trip was fun. But with every day that drew closer to their departure date, her anxiety had increased. And now the reality was they were on a highway in the northeastern corner of the United States, where they didn't know another living soul, heading to a town they had only pointed to on a globe and seen basic pictures of on the internet. Verity worried that this might just be the stupidest thing she had ever done. Second only to believing every word her husband, Sonny, had said to her as they stood at the altar in front of both sets of parents.

*To have and to hold from this day forward, for better, for worse, for richer, for poorer, in sickness and in health, till death us do part.*

*Or until a sharp-tongued food critic with big boobs, baby-doll eyes, and an insatiable appetite comes along, called Freya...*

She smiled to herself as she added the addendum. Not that she blamed Freya. Freya wasn't married to her, Sonny was. His reaction to them going away was typical. *How will you manage?* like she was a child who needed minding, and *Supposing I need something?* His selfishness and complete lack of faith in her ability to survive without him the cherry on the cake, in fact his words had only strengthened her resolve to make the trip as successful as it could be. To show him that she could not only survive but thrive!

'Mum?' Sophie raised her voice. 'I was asking you if you think we'll have good internet? I told Paloma and Eliza I'd Facetime them when I got there and let them have a look around, and also it's Darius's birthday on Saturday and I'm going to virtually attend his party. His parents are setting up a sushi bar in their basement. How cool is that?'

'Very.' Verity hated the big show of expense for birthdays. She and Sonny had never gone all out in that way, knowing it was the key to keeping their girl grounded when it would have been so easy to lob money in her direction. Particularly as it would have been a way to assuage the guilt she felt at working such long hours in their restaurant, meaning Sophie often had to fend for herself.

'Why the big sigh? What's wrong with sushi?' Her daughter's voice had gone up an octave as it did when she was agitated or spoiling for a fight.

'Nothing is wrong with sushi.' Verity paused, wondering if it were worth rocking the applecart this early on in proceedings, but deciding that, actually, it was important to set ground rules. 'It's not sushi I have a problem with. I love sushi! But I guess it's just that we are here in Vermont and it's our adventure, our escape, and I think we should really commit to it, throw ourselves into the community, and spend time together doing all the things we spoke about.'

'So, what are you saying? I can't speak to my friends

now?' Sophie laughed behind her words at the absurdity of the suggestion.

'No, of course you can speak to your friends, stay in touch with your friends, miss your friends… I guess what I'm saying is that I don't want you to yearn for your friends or spend your whole time virtually engaging with them because then you might as well as be at home with them. And if you long to be with them, that might feel like the worst of both worlds, not physically there to enjoy their company and not mentally here to enjoy our trip.'

''Kay.' Sophie sank down in the chair and Verity hated that this was the mood now set, the pattern too familiar: her reprimanding and Sophie closing down a little until time passed, the atmosphere settled, or the next event erased the sticky silence and topped up their happy. It was not how she wanted to arrive at their destination. Not at all.

'I think, I think Darius might like Eliza… and by like, I mean fancy.' Her child let this hang, as she stared out at the tree-lined horizon, where spikey green sentinels stood proudly along the ridge in the distance. Her words casual and yet her tone echoed with the longing and lamentation that every woman would recognize in her seventeen-year-old self. That single observation that had the power to shred the confidence of even the most outgoing spirit, when the object of your desire favoured another. Verity knew only too well what this felt like, and the shredding of her confidence, at forty-six, was a lot more recent.

'And do you *like* Darius?' she asked cautiously, trying to strike the right balance between being interested and prying, as she pictured the pretty boy with the cocky air and flashy wristwatch, the boy who would confidently open her fridge and hunt for snacks without asking, who seemed a lot more animated when Sophie's famous dad was around, and who, in her humble opinion, was not someone to trust with your heart.

'Mum, *everyone* likes Darius.' Sophie's mouth twisted in the beginnings of a smile.

'Of course they do.' He was *that* boy. She laughed and her daughter followed. It broke the tension, erased any awkwardness that lingered over their earlier exchange. 'I love you, Soph. I love you so much! I want this to be the best time for us. I can't stand the thought of coming all this way and it not being.'

'Mum, don't do what you always do, set a goal, a target, state that it has to be perfect, because nothing ever is, and then I know you're left feeling disappointed.'

'God!' Verity felt the words land like tiny daggers in her fragile breast, mainly because she knew it to be the truth. She also knew at some level that she wanted Sophie to return to the UK and tell Sonny they had had the best time, that her mum was fine, happy even! Because that would mean he hadn't won and that she had fooled Sophie at least that she wasn't entirely broken. It was selfish and petty, but nonetheless it was how she felt, and just the thought of this emotional subterfuge was enough to leave her feeling shredded by the loss of her marriage.

'I don't want to upset you!' Sophie twisted in her seat now to face her. 'I just want it to be the best time too and it *will* be if we just go with the flow!'

'You're right.' She took a deep breath and gripped the steering wheel. 'You are absolutely right, let's go with the flow, darling.'

The two sat in silence as they trundled on with the windows down a little and the warm New England breeze lifting their hair and their spirits. It sure was a beautiful part of the world, devoid of the cluttered buildings, crowds, and constant hum of noise that were familiar in London.

'Mum, look!' Sophie pointed at the sign that read "Welcome to Linden Falls."

'It's so pretty!' She spoke her initial thoughts aloud as they rolled into town, taking in the stunning, quaint pocket of Americana. 'Bertie's Petals,' she read aloud as they passed a florist with a stunning display. 'Cool name.' The town square was dominated by a large tree. White picket fences, painted frontages, flower-filled porches, neat pavements, and clapboard buildings lined Main Street. It was everything she had hoped it would be. She felt excitement swell in her veins.

'I just saw a bookshop!' Sophie squealed, as she turned to look out of the back window. 'Town Square Books!'

'Well, amen for that. If nothing else, we have books!' She smiled. How she loved that she and her girl shared a love of the written word, not that the restaurant had left her much time for reading in recent times. This holiday, however, was her chance to catch up on all the lovely novels that had caught her eye over the last year or so. Covers that enticed and left her with a longing to settle down in a quiet corner, lose herself in a jolly good tale under a soft blanket and with a decent cuppa in her hand. Picturing the business, she wondered, not for the first time, how Sonny and the team would manage without her for three whole months. It was conflicting; part of her wanted them to do well, and the other half wanted them to count down the days until she returned, quite unable to cope without her. And of course, this applied particularly to Sonny, who she wanted to want her, to fall into her arms and beg for forgiveness. As to whether she would forgive him or not, she was undecided. But still her heart flexed at the thought. This followed instantly by a hollow sadness that it was the case, wishing she were not still hankering for the man who had rejected her. It did nothing to raise her self-esteem.

'Right.' Sophie opened the notes on her phone and read the potted instructions the cabin owner, Mrs Mills, had sent. 'According to this, we go through the town and head out on the main route, we follow the road around, which climbs sharply, and take the second left when we see the sign for White Cedar Farm. We turn up the track and our cabin is the last one of three on the right. Key will be under the mat.'

Verity felt her gut bunch with excitement. 'Don't

you love that we are staying somewhere safe enough to leave a key under the mat?' She shook her head, trying to imagine doing something similar in London. The very idea was laughable. 'My parents used to do the same thing, in case they ever got locked out or if my sister or I came home unexpectedly, or they were taken ill. An ex-police officer neighbour of theirs told them it was a crackers idea, that they might have been in the sedate suburbs of Harrow but were no less prone to burglars. He frightened them half to death.'

'What did they do?'

'They did the obvious thing—moved the key from under the mat to the flowerpot by the front door, confident no one would *ever* think of looking in there!' She laughed at the memory and wished, as she sometimes did, that she could go back, just for an hour or two, to that simple time of childhood. The days when her mum baked cakes that they ate in their leafy back garden while her dad pruned the roses and her sister blew and chased bubbles, laughing at the delicate rainbow orbs that hinted at magic as they floated over the trimmed privet hedge. Not a day passed when she didn't miss her dad so much that it was almost painful to remember him. Her tears gathered, as they did when she thought of him, wondering if the longing for him would ever diminish. It was a weird thing, but Sonny's infidelity had angered her on her dad's behalf, knowing that, were he still alive, he would have been so disappointed in the man he had called son. That and the fact that both of the men she had loved and relied on had, for very different reasons, abandoned her in a little under twenty-four months.

The trees grew thicker now and the view down over the winding valley more spectacular. Slowly she navigated the lane. The road twisted to the right, meaning they had almost the perfect view of Linden Falls in front of them.

'Here, Mum!' Sophie sat forward and pointed to a gap in the bend and a carved wooden sign that read "White Cedar Farm." A less discerning eye would have missed it altogether. Verity turned expertly from the main road.

The track was rock-covered, and pothole strewn, but the chunky off-roader navigated the terrain with ease. Verity laughed and Sophie joined in, as much in nervous anticipation of what they might find at the end of the road as the fact that they jiggled all over the place.

*I wish you could see us, Sonny. We have arrived and I'm coping well—on the surface at least. I'm driving on the wrong side of the road... We are in Vermont! Doing just fine without you... and I wish... I wish I didn't think about you every time there is a space in my thoughts. I wish you were not in my thoughts at all... I wish I didn't conjure images of you and Freya Walsh and you making her laugh the way you used to me... getting up in the wee, small hours to make her toast and honey the way you did me... making her promises that you won't keep, like you did me...*

'Oh my God, it's so cute!' Her daughter's enthusiasm for the place they were to stay drew her from her thoughts.

They drove past the first of three wooden cabins. Piled logs made up the walls, and the roof was a neat triangle with the stovepipe for a log burner standing proud in one corner. The front door was recessed inside a wide porch, and in pride of place sat two vintage Adirondack chairs whose pale green paint had faded a little.

The second cabin was set back even farther. Neither showed any signs of life and both were entirely private, situated in their own generous, tree-lined plots. Finally, they spied their home for the next three months. Set high at the top of the field, it was very much like the other two cabins, but the extra bedroom gave it a different configuration, almost with a wing on the right-hand side. With the handbrake on, they abandoned the car and stood with hands on hips to admire the timber building.

'Wowsers!' Verity hid her alarm. It was hard to tell from the outside, but she was trying to figure whether it was going to be homely or a horror story inside. Her gut shrank, as she kicked at the muddy coir welcome mat and retrieved the clunky key, noting the shape it left in the dust, and wondering how long it was since the cabin had been rented and whether anyone had thought to air the place. She offered up a silent prayer, which was not unusual of late, but this one was a little different.

*Please let there be clean sheets, hot water, and a fridge... oh, and coffee would be most welcome.*

The front door was constructed of rough wood with old iron door furniture and a small bull's-eye glass window with a red-and-white gingham curtain behind it. She put the key in the door and eased it open, listening with alarm to the creak that sounded a lot like the reluctant wakening of a long-slumbering thing across the floor. Her breath came easily, and the relief was instant. Inside, the cabin was nothing short of beautiful. Open plan and with an abundance of wood, including two baskets of logs piled high beside the log burner. Flagstone floors were covered in a delightful array of handwoven rugs, and the cushions on the cane sofas were brightly embroidered, providing pops of colour that lifted the whole place.

On an oversized dresser sat a stack of board games. The boxes were less than pristine and all the more enticing for it. It was easy to picture families and couples sitting at the scrubbed wooden table and laughing by candlelight as they clashed over Scrabble and Uno. The interior was worn, homely, and permeated with the scent of woodsmoke and memories, the kind that embed themselves in the walls when the occupants are reluctant to lock up and leave, giving one last look and offering a silent promise of return. Promises that now hovered in the pine-scented atmosphere and nestled on the rafters.

Sophie raced ahead and up the small stairway that led to a sleeping loft at the far end of the cabin, the vast bed with its red and green tapestry cover visible from the front door.

'Can I sleep up here? It's amazing! It's like a little flat of my own. I love it!'

'Sure, you can.' Verity beamed at her daughter's delight, matched only by her own enthusiasm for the small counter that constituted a kitchen, where hand-made cupboard doors of old pine sat beneath a stun-ning slice of oak on which she found a not-so-fancy coffee machine, but it would do. Coffee was coffee, right? A microwave oven, a two-ring stove, and below that a humming fridge.

Cautiously she opened the door to what would, by default, be her room. It was square with a glorious brass bed covered in a patchwork quilt that was soft to the touch. It had more plump pillows than she needed, propped against the tarnished bedstead, and the temp-tation to fall onto it and sleep was strong. Jet lag and the effects of the long drive were beginning to bite.

She knew, however, that the worst thing to do would be give in to it, as that could throw you off course for days. Best to do as she and Sonny had always done when travelling—soldier on and only sleep when bedtime came. If she could last that long. Wide French doors provided the main feature of the space, which she threw open, standing back to take in the incredible vista from her own private deck, on which sat two sturdy rocking chairs placed at angles. It was like a painting. Trees lined the valley in a wide sweep that went all the way down to a lake, where she could make out boats crisscrossing the water, cutting their way through the sea diamonds that danced on the surface. The variegated greens of the towering spikey evergreens sat against the blue sky, and with warm air still and sweet, she thought this might just be paradise. It was exactly what she needed, this peace, this time to mentally regroup. This quiet...

'Hello?' a woman's low voice called from the front porch, drawing her from her thoughts.

'Oh, hi!' she called in return as she smoothed her hair and pinched her cheeks, remembering how Sonny used to say she looked like a harassed scarecrow after any travel.

'Mrs Joseph! Welcome to Linden Falls! I'm Leona Mills. Please call me Leo. We've emailed a few times.'

'Yes, of course, Leo.' She studied the petite woman, who she estimated to be in her mid-sixties. She had the tan, makeup-free face of someone who lived an outdoors kind of life, her dark hair, streaked with grey, was secured into a loose plait, and her eyes were of the palest blue and smiled even when her face was resting. Her jeans were worn on the knees, her boots heavy and functional, and her grey linen shirt thin from wear. Verity liked her on sight. 'And please call me Verity. We've only just arrived. The place is lovely! Just lovely! Thank you so much.' She checked the emotion that caused her eyes to water. A combination no doubt of relief to have someone like Leo, who owned the cabins, check in, joy at the glorious place she was to call home for a while, and the echo of sadness, her hurt still fresh at the fact that Sonny had discarded her.

'Well, that makes me happy.' Leo spoke slowly, as if she had all the time in the world, and after the hectic pace of life in Chelsea, where everyone seemed to be in a rush, Verity found it appealing. 'I brought you this.'

Leo handed her a wicker shopping basket with a warm, whole wheat loaf poking from the top, a glass jar full of jam the colour of rubies, and four of the fattest, reddest apples she had ever seen. Her mouth watered.

'Oh, Leo! Thank you!'

'No problem and there's fresh milk, butter, and orange juice in the fridge.' She pointed in the unlikely event her guest was yet to locate the small kitchenette. 'And there's ground coffee in the tin.'

'I can't thank you enough. That's perfect and so kind!' She meant it.

'Hi, Mrs Mills! I'm Sophie!'

Verity watched with pride as her daughter rattled down the stairs from the bed deck and introduced herself.

'Welcome, Sophie. You like bird-watching?'

'I've never done it.' Sophie exchanged a glance with her mum; the opportunities for bird-watching in central London and with their busy schedule were a little thin on the ground.

'Well, my husband, Walt, is bird mad! And I'm thankful not only for his hobby but because it gets him out from under my feet.' She pulled a face and Sophie laughed. 'He's always looking for a day trip buddy if you don't mind an early start and getting your boots muddy.'

'I'll think about it.' Sophie nodded. 'Thank you.'

'So polite.' Leo spoke as if to herself.

'Are the other cabins occupied?' Verity was curious.

'One, yes, a long-term resident like yourselves: Mr Darby. And the other, the first cabin you pass on the way in, tends to be weekend rentals, city folk who need to detox a little.'

'Well, I can see why they'd choose here. It's so peaceful. Beautiful.'

Leo nodded her agreement and took a deep breath, as if the air itself was nectar. 'Listen, I'll leave you to get settled, but if you need anything, you have my cell number, and Walt and I are only five minutes away up at the top of the ridge.' She pointed behind her. 'The grocery mart is in town and there's Doc's Fountain, which does the best coffee, and a beauty salon, where Vera can fix all your beauty needs. She's a magician. She has a phrase, what is it now...' Leo clicked her fingers as if this might aid her memory, 'aint nothing a little curl and lipstick can't cure!' she chuckled and ran her palm over her make-up free face.

Verity touched her own thick locks, wondering if it was a hint.

'And there's the bookstore, which is owned and run by my friend, Margot—her daughter, Paige, is there now too. The deli is a delight, oh, and Woody makes the best pizza. And that's before you see our famous Wishing Tree.'

Verity and Sophie exchanged a look. *Okaaaay...*

Leo continued as if nothing was amiss, 'So there's plenty to explore. Call if you need anything or have any questions, anything at all.' She spoke with her palms open and her eyes wide; her sincerity and kindness were evident.

'I have a question, Mrs Mills!' Sophie piped up, almost jumping on the spot, as if her request was urgent and she was worried Leo might leave without giving her the chance to ask, 'What's the Wi-Fi code?'

'Wi-Fi code?' Leo looked a little perplexed.

'For the internet? For my laptop and my phone, so I can, you know, Facetime my friends and stuff.' Her tone was a little rushed. Verity noted how her daughter avoided her eye contact, more than aware that this request would be a little disappointing.

'Oh, there's no internet signal here. You're lucky to get cell phone coverage half the time, but you can get a good reception in town. I see a lot of the kids on the benches in the town square. All tip tapping away instead of talkin' to each other! And we have Wi-Fi up at the farmhouse. If you need to send an email or it's urgent, come sit on our porch—any time. You'd be most welcome.'

'So, I can't... I mean... I usually... It's just that there's a thing...' Sophie ran out of words.

'Mrs Mills has very kindly said you can sit on her

porch and use her internet,' Verity reminded her, a little sternly.

'Yes.' Her daughter found the beginnings of a smile. 'Thank you.'

'And thank you for our goodies!' She raised the basket. 'Didn't realise I was hungry until I smelled this bread. I might eat the lot.'

Leo looked her up and down, and Verity suspected that a friend would have commented that it would be no bad thing. She knew she was a little on the skinny side. Heartache, feeling a little less than adequate when comparing herself to her husband's paramour, and her subsequent loss of appetite would do that.

# CHAPTER 2

*J*t took Verity a second after opening her eyes to remember where she was. Instinctively she had reached out to lay her hand on Sonny's chest, to touch his back, graze his arm, the feel of him before she greeted the day enough to reassure her that all was well in her world. Her palm fell onto the cool white sheet, and it was this that jolted her awake. This tiny act, a daily and startling reminder that they had parted. The flickering melancholy was, however, easy to relegate to the back of her mind when she sat up and looked out though the French windows at the view on this, their second day in Linden Falls.

After clambering from the high brass bed, she threw open the doors and drank in the sight of the sun glinting on the lake in the distance and the light breaking over the trees, covering the world in a golden glaze. Her stomach rumbled with hunger. They had devoured the bread and jam for supper, washed down with sharp iced orange juice—a blissful, simple meal that had deliciously sated their hunger. After sitting in the rocking chairs wrapped in quilts, drinking in the silence, and watching the sun slip beyond the horizon, they had waltzed off to bed. Verity had certainly slept soundly for the first time in weeks, this alone enough to restore some of her well-being.

The not-so-fancy coffee machine on the counter made a decent enough cup, and with Sophie snoring from the sleeping loft, she took her morning brew out onto the front porch. Staring up at the big sky, she raised her middle finger high. *That's for you, Sonny! I hope London is hot and noisy, I hope you had trouble finding a parking spot, I hope your salad delivery has wilted, and I hope you wish you were here!* She did a little dance, spinning around with her eyes closed and her free arm raised before plopping down on the wide front step with her nightdress wrapped around her legs and her pashmina about her shoulders to ward off the chill where the sun was yet to reach.

'Morning.'

'Oh!' She hadn't meant to yell the word, but jumped, spilling coffee down her front. It was as shocking as it was embarrassing to see a man coming from the forest to the side of their plot, that and she was still in her nightwear, whereas he had clearly been up for some time, as per the backpack over his shoulder, the heavy breathing of someone who had hiked up the hillside, and the fact that he was most definitely not in his pyjamas.

'I tried to make a noise so as not to scare you, but you were…' He looked skyward, and his mouth moved wordlessly, as if unsure of how to phrase what he had seen.

'I was just…' She too faltered.

'It doesn't matter. I…' He took a beat and the awkwardness seemed to dissipate. 'I'm your neighbour.'

'Mr Darby?'

'Yes.' His voice was gravelly, gruff yet quiet, with a rasp that suggested it wasn't overly used.

'I wasn't expecting someone to come out of the woods!'

'I can see that.' His words might have been comedic were it not for his rather stern stance.

'It's nice to dance in the sunlight—makes you feel good.'

He stared at her, his expression quizzical.

'All right then.' He gave a small nod and walked past, as if neither what made her feel good nor her presence in her nightgown was of any consequence to him. Quickening his pace, he disappeared down the track, heading no doubt to his cabin.

'*Nice to dance in the sunlight*. Why in the world did you say *that*? You sounded like a total weirdo!' she whispered to herself.

'Did you just shout?' Sophie sauntered onto the deck, yawning and stretching her skinny arms over her head without any sense of urgency.

'Yes! But the time it's taken you to come to my

rescue, it's of no matter. Anything could have happened to your poor, defenseless mother!'

'Why did you yell?' Her daughter yawned again and rubbed her eyes. 'It woke me up.'

'So sorry about that, dear, but a man came out of the trees.' She pointed to where he had emerged.

Sophie laughed loudly. 'God, Mother, that sounds so dramatic! A man came out of the trees!' she mimicked her. 'Was he carrying an axe?'

'No, a knapsack.'

'Well, no wonder you screamed!' Sophie sank down beside her on the step. 'Where is he now?'

'He's gone. It was our neighbour, Mr Darby.'

'So, what's he like?'

'Hard to say.' She sipped her coffee. 'Outdoorsy, a bit cowboyish, quiet or moody, I'm not sure which, and not what you'd call overly chatty. Think he'd been on an early-morning jaunt.'

'And by cowboyish, you mean he was wearing a Stetson? Had a lasso in his hand? Trailing a horse? Leather chaps?' Sophie asked comically.

'No, not quite. He was wearing jeans and a plaid shirt.'

'That doesn't make him a cowboy, Mummy.'

'Well, whatever he is, I doubt we will see much of him and that suits me just fine. We're not here to make friends; we are here to spend time together. Talking of which, how about we go into town today, pick up some groceries, visit the bookstore, get our bearings?'

'Yes! I'll shower after you.' Sophie jumped up. 'And I can Facetime Paloma and Eliza while we're out!'

Verity closed her eyes and breathed slowly, wishing her daughter's glee for the trip was not, as she suspected, because it gave her access to the world across the pond they were supposed to be taking a break from.

Her own shower was powerful and brief. The only way to ensure there was enough hot water for them both. With their hair damp about their shoulders and none of the preparation that would see them ready for a jaunt up the Kings Road on a sunny day, the two buckled up, and with a heady excitement to explore their new surroundings and the scent of summer air filling the car, they trundled into town.

Having parked the car, Verity looked around. Instantly, she liked the quaintness of the place, the cutesy shopfronts, the flowering baskets hanging from lampposts, and the smiley, waving nature of the neighbours who heralded each other from across the street. It had a community feel that was missing in her corner of London, where life was fast and impersonal, where screens were ever pressed to noses, and where everyone seemed to be running just to stand still.

'Hello.' The young woman who was pouring coffee into a mug smiled as she and Sophie entered Town Square Books.

'Hi!' Sophie waved. 'I like your sign and I like your red door.'

'Thanks.' The woman smiled as if the compliment meant the world. 'My dad made it a long time ago now.'

'He sure did!' an older lady called from the chair in the corner, where she sat with a book on her lap, disturbed no doubt at the mention of her sign.

'Well, he did a good job.'

The older woman beamed at the compliment.

Verity carefully stepped over a snoozing golden retriever who was sprawled in front of the U-shaped counter. 'We're staying up at White Cedar Farm, in one of Leo's cabins.'

The girl sipped her drink and nodded, as the older woman shouted out, 'Leo and I are old friends. I'm Margot. This is Paige, my daughter'—the girl raised her hand in a wave—'and that sleeping hound at your feet is Gladys.'

Verity laughed as the dog snored, unperturbed by their presence. 'Well, I'm Verity and this is Sophie.'

'Good to meet you.' Margot smiled. 'Holler if you need any help.'

'Thank you.' Verity smiled.

'That's not a local accent. Where're you guys from?' Margot asked.

'England. London.'

The woman nodded, suggesting she had suspected as much. 'Yes, of course, I heard Leo had some British guests coming in.'

'That's us!' Rather than take umbrage at the fact that their arrival was gossip, it instead made her feel welcome. 'Only arrived last night and we are in dire need of books and breakfast.'

'Well, you're in the right place, and I can help you with at least one of those.' The woman smiled warmly, and Verity liked her instantly.

'Hey, Sophie. Do you like to read?' Paige asked.

'Sometimes. I never know what to pick though.' Her daughter blushed, looking very much like her little girl and not the leggy teen that had inhabited her body for the past few years. Sophie's awkwardness sent a bolt of love right through Verity's core.

'But I'm guessing you like a good story?' Paige was kind, patient. Sophie nodded. 'Have you read the Twilight series by Stephanie Meyer?'

'I saw half of the first film. It was at my friend's sleepover, but I haven't read the books.'

'Well, why don't you try the first one. There's a lot more in the books than was in the movie, and if you like it, there's a whole series.'

'Have you read them?' Sophie asked.

Paige leaned forward, adding a certain air of conspiracy to the whole exchange. 'I have, and I loved them. I've reread them twice.'

'Okay. I'll give them a go, thank you.'

Verity was proud of her daughter's politeness until, in the next breath, Sophie called over her shoulder, 'Mum, can you get me the first one? I just need to go outside and get a signal. I promised Paloma and Eliza…' and with that she was gone.

Verity let out a long sigh. 'I wish that damned phone would drop down a well!'

Paige laughed and Margot nodded, as if understanding the many trials of motherhood.

'No, seriously, we are here on this extended holiday and the idea is to spend time together, but she's more interested in connecting with her friends and virtually attending a birthday party in London, if you can believe that?' It was a weird thing, but she suddenly felt quite alone. As if Sophie was only going through the motions, keen to get home, Sonny was living it up in London with his sexy food critic, and what was she doing? Standing in a bookstore with a stranger, wondering where she might find Edward Cullen lurking...

'Would you like some tea?'

Verity had zoned out and stared now at Margot. 'I'm sorry?'

'Tea?' She pointed to a kettle.

'Oh! Bless you. I'd love a tea! And sorry for being miles away. I have a lot going on.'

'Don't we all.' Paige gave a wry smile in her mother's direction, and Verity realised in that second that she was short of friends. A life of working such ridiculously long shifts, seven days a week, made it hard to be a perky member of a friendship group. That and her friends had not been overly keen on Sonny. Not that their views had influenced her either way, she'd still married the man, but it did make it a little harder to all meet up for supper and make small talk when she knew they were less than approving of her husband, whose star was rapidly rising. She wondered what they might be making of the latest news and how long before they made contact.

The bookstore was well stocked and there were chairs for readers to sink into. The atmosphere was unhurried and welcoming. The kind of place she could see herself idling the hours away.

Margot placed the teacup in front of her on a table, and a small plate with not one but two fat cinnamon rolls sitting on it. Verity felt her mouth water, realising that it had been a while since they had polished off the warm bread and jam for supper. She took a large bite and let the icing, sugar, and cinnamon-dusted crumbs fall down her shirt.

'Oh, that's so good!' she mouthed, closing her eyes, as her discerning palette identified the flavours. 'Sweet, cinnamon, a hint of vanilla, and something else... what is that?'

'I'm afraid if you want the answer to that you'll have to sneak into the Cobblestone Bakery when they're making them.' She winked. 'Did you think they were homemade? I mean, who could replicate these at home?'

*I could...* She thought of her time on the pastry section of the restaurant and, as was often the case, felt floored by the recollection.

She cursed the tears that pooled. 'Oh! Sorry! My eyes are a bit leaky.'

'Grab a napkin, Paige!' Margot called out. 'That's okay, honey, you let it out.' Paige handed her a napkin.

'We're not only here on an extended holiday; we're kind of escaping from the world as well. Or at least I am,' she babbled.

'Well, it's as good a place as any. And I should know.' Paige looked out of the window at the pretty town.

Verity wondered what her story was. 'It's funny, isn't it? I thought coming far away meant I might leave any sadness behind. Turns out I might have inadvertently packed it with my toothbrush and pyjamas and brought it with me!' she joked, trying simultaneously to lighten the mood and to paint herself in a less gloomy light to the mother and daughter who had been so lovely.

'Sounds like you might need a trip to the Wishing Tree.'

'The what?' Verity sipped her tea and thought she might have misheard.

Margot pulled up a chair. 'You see that big old linden tree in the middle of the square?'

Verity turned and took in the impressive ancient elder statesman, which was covered in fairy lights that she bet looked very pretty when darkness fell. 'Yes.'

'Well, the belief is that it can grant wishes.'

Paige rolled her eyes and disappeared through a door into the main building.

'Oh, right, Leo might have might have mentioned it. We thought she must be joking!'

'Folks come from miles around just to tie their deepest, darkest desire on the branches. It's a pretty sight, a little sad too, all those ribbons, notes, and messages blowing in the breeze, placed by people looking for something, hoping for something...' Margot spoke quietly, her voice a little thin, and Verity wondered what *she* might be looking for, hoping for, planning for, or regretting, not that they were well acquainted enough for her to ask.

'But it's just a gimmick, right?' She gave a nervous laugh at the absurdity of the woman's suggestion. 'Something to woo the tourists?'

'It depends on who you ask. We have couples turn up with much-wished-for babies who they have named Linden. We have women wearing wedding bands who had put the call out for Mr Right, and we have the elderly who might have visited decades ago and asked for no more than a long and happy life... so, I don't know!' She let her palms rise and fall against the table-top. 'What I can say is that it's always been kind to me, but there are times when it hasn't.' Her response was vague.

'Well, good luck to all those people, but I don't think it's for me,' she tittered a little awkwardly, imagining what Sonny would say: *Utterly bonkers!*

'Well, that's fine too, although it seems to me you might already have told me what you'd wish for,'

'I did?' *For my husband to come back, for him to ditch Freya and pick me...* The thought leapt into her mind, and she wondered how Margot knew.

'For your daughter's phone to drop down a well?'

Margot laughed softly. Of course, *that* was what she was talking about. Verity joined in, as much with relief as anything else.

With her tea drunk, one fat cinnamon roll devoured, a book purchased, and the buds of friendship starting to bloom, Verity left the bookstore with a promise to return.

Margot was right, the Wishing Tree was beautiful, an ancient linden with wide, abundant branches and the flutter of all those hopes and dreams gently blowing in the wind. Looking over her shoulder to make sure no one was watching, she carefully took the lid off the black felt-tipped pen and reached for one of the labels, pre-tied with ribbon that sat in an old wooden box. She hesitated. It was actually a lot harder than she thought, to succinctly put down her deepest wants and display it for the world to see, albeit anonymously.

The pen seemed to hover over the paper for an age, and she wondered whether it might be easier to simply abandon the idea altogether. Verity adjusted her sunglasses, and the memories of the night Sonny left came clear and fast. Again, she heard the sound of the front door clicking shut, saw his holdall haphazardly stuffed with underwear, grabbed by the handful from the drawer, his toothbrush in his pocket, leaving hers alone in the ceramic holder by the sink, abandoned. Shirts and trousers on hangers, dangling from his fingers and slung over his shoulder. He never looked back but quickened his pace on the stairs, seemingly keen to escape the place and go grab the new life he was creating for himself. She recalled the ache for him deep in her gut, the absent shape of him, the dent of his head on the pillow, the scent of him on the sheets, and the way her tears trickled in a hot spring of despair, over her temple and into the pillowslip, as she pictured him with Freya Walsh. And suddenly, words flowed from her like poetry from the mouth of the suffering:

*I wish... I wish Sonny still wanted me... I wish I could start over, restored and happy... I wish my heart would stop hurting... I wish to be loved!*

Reaching for the ribbon, she bent low and placed it discreetly on a busy lower branch, hiding it from view and breathing in an erratic rhythm as embarrassment clung to her skin. She watched for a second, saw it dancing with its neighbours in the wind, giving her a moment of hope. Looking skyward now, she put her hand on her brow to shield her eyes from the light, as if believing that, if she looked hard enough, she might see her words spiralling upwards, preparing to make their way across the water and land in her husband's ear.

'Looks like it might rain.'

She hadn't noticed the older lady with a stunning mane of long, silver hair, softly caught at the nape of her neck, now standing by her side and who too was looking up.

Verity stared at the paper messages and a small laugh escaped her mouth. 'Well, I guess that's the end of my wish then. One fat raindrop and the whole thing will be illegible!'

'That's why I'm here.' The woman looked her up and down. 'I'm Neva Cabot, and I run the Wishing Tree Inn right across the street.'

Verity looked over at the bed-and-breakfast.

'And if the weather turns, I gather all the wishes and keep them safe.'

'Wow! That's quite a responsibility.' Verity loved that Neva bothered to do this.

'Been doing it for more years now than I care to count. I catalogue them and store them away.'

'I don't know what to say, except thank you. I mean, I don't know you, but thank you. I think it's a wonderful thing to do. I'm Verity Joseph, here with my daughter, Sophie.'

'The Curator of Wishes, that's what they call me,' Neva announced with pride before retuning her gaze to the sky and the dark cloud that seemed to be passing right on by without so much as a drop of rain. 'I'll keep an eye on it. Watch out for rain.' She smiled and made her way back to her inn. 'And welcome to Linden Falls. How's the cabin working out?'

'Oh!' She was taken aback again that nothing seemed to be secret in this place. 'It's beautiful.'

Neva had her hands in the pocket of her parka, and suddenly she pulled out something shiny, holding it up to examine it.

'Well, I'll be. I know this wasn't in here that last time I wore this. I think maybe it's for you.'

'For me?' Verity laughed nervously.

Neva held out the object.

It was neon green, with a little rust around the metal hooks.

'A fishing lure?'

'I know. I'm surprised too,' Neva said. 'Must've belonged to my late brother as I've never been a fisher-woman. Now it's yours.'

'Oh. Well. Thank you,' Verity mumbled with embarrassment as she took it into her hands.

'It has a thingie that you can use to put it on your belt loop. I'm sure you'll find a use for it. Here, let me help.' Neva fastened the lure to Verity's jeans, making quite an awkward moment, then smiled her approval before disappearing inside.

'Mum!' Sophie stood out to her, even at a distance as she walked toward the square from the other side of the street. She quickly forgot about the old lure, as her heart flexed with love for the beautiful, exasperating human she had grown.

'I spoke to Paloma and Eliza was at her house. They were going to get their nails done and then they're meeting the guys.'

Verity saw her stare at her own nails and bite the side of her cheek. She knew Sophie would be feeling a little left out, a little envious.

'Have you seen the tree?' She tried for distraction, her ally when she was wanting for words of solace.

'Isn't it the coolest?' Her daughter's dark brown eyes widened as she took in the spreading branches.

'I guess. Great for tourists and a bit of fun,' Verity added, a little dismissively.

'Well, lucky us then, as we are tourists who want a bit of fun! Shall we make a wish?'

Verity looked away, knowing her disingenuousness would be easier if she wasn't looking directly at her daughter. 'I don't think so, darling.'

'Well, I might.' Sophie put her finger on her lips as she did when she was thinking. 'But not now, not with you standing right there. It has to be a secret, right?'

She had to admit that Sophie's enthusiasm for the task was a little infectious.

'Yes, it definitely has to be a secret. Now come on, let's get back to the cabin. We have books to read! And I might have picked up some truffled mac and cheese from the Crooked Porch Café and a tub of coleslaw.' She raised the bag with the goodies inside.

'Good, I'm starving!' Sophie's familiar refrain.

It amazed her how quickly she had got used to driving the hire car and how comfortable she was on the streets of Linden Falls.

'Who was that older lady you were talking to? She had great hair!'

'Didn't she just. Her name's Neva Cabot and she's the Curator of Wishes, no less.'

'Wowsers, that's some title. Bet the printer did a double take when he was asked to print those business cards.' Sophie giggled.

'She seemed nice.' Verity felt kindly toward the woman who did such a wonderful thing.

'I liked Paige and Margot too.' Sophie flicked

through the *Twilight* paperback her mum had treated her to.

'And me. Anyone who gives me tea and cinnamon buns is all right by me.' She meant it, plus it felt nice to know there were people in town she could wave to or call upon, familiar.

'Did you tell them about you and Dad?'

She could feel her daughter's eyes staring at her, no doubt waiting to gauge her reaction at the mention of her husband. Sophie's fingers were now still on the book.

'No. Didn't think it was the right thing for a first meeting, to overshare with strangers that my heart has recently dissolved.'

'Your heart's dissolved?' There was an unmistakable note of horror in her Sophie's tone. 'Oh, Mum!'

Verity cursed herself for having spoken so freely. 'No! Not dissolved.' She tutted, backtracking. 'I'm just being dramatic. My heart's more bruised, a little knocked out of shape, but no long-term damage done, I'm sure of it. I'll bounce back, Soph, eventually.'

'I can't stand to think of you hurt, Mummy.' The tremor to her voice was heartbreaking.

'You don't have to worry about me, sweetheart. It's just life! Things happen that pull the rug from under your feet, and you fall so hard it leaves you winded, but it's all part of the rich tapestry and it makes you resilient, toughens you up. And it will be the case for you too. Even though this whole thing is between Dad and me, you're inevitably caught in the crossfire a little, and it will change the shape of you too. And I can't stand to think of that. Because you were so very happy, living a great life without too much to worry about. I feel like we've spoiled it for you.'

Sophie placed the book inside its bag and took a slow breath. 'You haven't spoiled things for me. I wasn't so very happy, Mum.'

'You weren't?' This was news.

'Well, I mean, I was happy, I *am* happy, but I didn't think you and Dad were and that worried me. I used to think about it before I fell asleep.'

'Why didn't you think we were happy?' The thought that Sophie had seen more clues than she made her heart race, dissolved or not.

Her daughter took her time and Verity took her foot off the gas, not wanting the journey to end before Sophie had said all that she wanted to, knowing that the confines of the car were a safe space for honesty, without interruption or distraction, and no need to look at each other directly.

'You know that picture of you and Daddy on Gordon's yacht in Cornwall?'

'Yes.' The silver-framed photograph sat in pride of place on the bookshelf in the sitting room. Sonny liked guests to notice it so he could regale them with snippets of the most perfect day: *the gentle swell of the ocean, the warmth of the sun on their skin, and the best bavette steak sandwich he had ever tasted, flashed over hot coals and slathered with French mustard before being shoved inside a fresh baguette.* The bite of it lived with him still apparently. She could see he loved hobnobbing with his celebrity mate in such opulence, whereas if she thought about that day, she only remembered feeling a little out of her depth, her sandals rubbing her heels, and trying not to give in to seasickness as the big old boat rode the waves. 'What about it?'

'Dad's face'—Sophie hesitated—'he looks like there's nowhere else he would rather be.'

'He's very fond of Gordon.'

'No,' her daughter interrupted, shaking her curly head. 'It's more than that. I see you look like that too sometimes, usually when someone compliments your food, but never when you're together.'

'I...' She tried to find the words, to phrase the explanation, the placatory sentence that meant reassurance, but there were none. This truth was as jarring as it was painful. 'We used to love being together, every second of every day.' Her mind flitted to when they had first opened the restaurant and excitement and adrenaline meant sleep was often relegated in the face of painting walls, scrubbing floors, securing suppliers, sampling produce, kissing, and drinking red wine on the floor of their very own eatery. It was a dream come true, a time when happiness outweighed their fatigue. 'But then we got so busy, and the years ran into one another, and Dad's career rocketed, and a month ago I learned I was not enough.'

'So, are you saying it was enough for you, Mum? The restaurant, Dad, that busy life?'

It was easy to forget this was her seventeen-year-old daughter talking and not a wise old friend with a treasure trove of sage advice. Verity took her time in responding.

'When I was growing up, my parents had rose-flowered wallpaper in their sitting room. Mum loved it, Dad hated it, and I didn't notice it, not after a while. It was just there, the background paper to our meals, rows, and laughter, and one day, I came home, and Mum had got the decorators in, and the walls were painted in a pale duck-egg blue. The room looked huge and fresh and so clean! It was a transformation, a revelation! And I wondered why we hadn't done it years ago. I guess Sonny and I were like that, old wallpaper. So much part of the fabric of everyday life you don't question it, don't see it, and now'—she lowered the window and breathed in the sweet New England air—'I'm getting used to the new view, but I'm still undecided if I like it, whether I'm happy for the chance to start over, or whether I miss my old life so much I doubt the lump in my throat will ever shift.'

'I really, really hope you come to love the new view, Mum. I want you both to be happy.'

'I know, sweet girl. Do you think Dad's happy now? Happier?'

Sophie nodded in her peripheral vision. 'I think he is. He looks like he does in that photograph. And he was saying on the phone that he wants to take me to St. Lucia at Christmas. Grandma Netta wants to see me. I said I'd think about it. I wanted to talk to you before I said yes or no.'

'Is he taking Freya too?' She thought of him arriving on the island and being greeted by his large and loving family with Freya in tow… her drinking a cold Piton beer while Sonny's mum whipped up her famous green figs and salt fish. The image was clear and left her feeling replaced and redundant. The thought alone knocked the breath from her. It hurt. Verity listened as her daughter carefully couched her reply.

'I think so, but I'm not sure. I'd have to check.'

'Well, of course you should go with them. Your dad gets so little time off and it's good you spend time with him, plus it's been a couple of years since you've been back. Grandma Netta won't believe how tall you are and those long, long legs of yours.' She smiled as broadly as she was able at her beautiful girl.

'I love you, Mummy.'

'And I love you.'

Verity could only grip the steering wheel, staring ahead. She welcomed the truthful exchange, yet now she pictured her wish hanging on that stupid bloody tree and ironically wished she could rip it down and shred it into a million pieces. Its very existence made her feel foolish. Sonny was happier without her, happier in his new life, and there wasn't a damned thing she could do about that.

They continued the rest of the journey in silence until she turned onto the rutted track, already learning to turn the wheel a little to the left or right to avoid the potholes, the positions of which were becoming familiar. Mr Darby was unloading the back of his pickup.

'He's seen us. I'd better go and say hi.' She reconciled her thoughts that she ought to be neighbourly. After Verity parked the car, Sophie ran into the house with her phone in her hand, probably to text her dad and say that she had the green light for Christmas in St. Lucia. Verity pictured their house in Chelsea over the festive period with just Wordsworth the cat for company. It would be fine. She'd make it fine.

With her keys in her hand, she backtracked until she was outside Mr Darby's cabin.

'Oh, you've been fishing?' Verity spied his catch, resting in a bunch on the end of a pole. The fish were neatly tied. Their iridescent skin shone in the sunlight, which picked up beautiful tones of mink and brown. They stared at her with wide, glassy eyes, the stillness of which made her want to weep at their demise.

'Uh-huh.' Rummaging around into the back of his pickup, he pulled out a battered cool box before reaching for a tarpaulin.

'So where do you fish?'

'Anywhere there's water.' He cast a cursory glance in her direction.

'Right. And I wanted to say, as we are going to be neighbours, I'm Verity.'

He stopped sorting out the tarpaulin. 'Verty?'

'Ve-ri-tee,' she enunciated.

'S'what I said, Verty,' he repeated.

'Well, that's close enough.' She laughed nervously. 'And you are?'

'Jack.' He adjusted his cap and she saw more of his face. A nice face when it gave her a little attention.

'Lovely to meet you, Jack, properly and not just the weird thing this morning when I was, erm…'

He stared at her a little quizzically and said nothing. She bit her lip as if this might stop her babbling. She remembered the lure and unbuckled it from her belt loop before holding it out.

'Maybe you can use this?'

He examined it. 'A vintage glowworm cone tail. Looks like a Heddon. You fish?'

She chuckled. 'No. Not at all. I…well, it's not actually mine—'

'Don't tell me, you ran into Neva Cabot.'

She smiled. 'I did, and I have no idea why she gave the lure thing to me.'

He stared at it before tucking it into his front pocket.

Verity looked around them, taking in the serene setting.

'So, you live up here? It's a beautiful place. Very different in the winter, I've heard.'

'Yup.' Again, he offered little by way of conversation.

'Well…' She paused, wondering if he might interject. He didn't. 'I'll leave you to it. *Great* chat!' she added with a large dollop of sarcasm and a double thumbs-up before turning on her heel and making her way to her cabin. She stopped at the front door and kicked off her boots, rubbing at the sole of her foot, which was a little sore.

'Were you talking to the cowboy?' Sophie called from the sofa on which she now lounged.

'No, I wasn't. He's not a cowboy; he's a moody fisherman. *Impossible* to chat to. I've tried to be neighbourly, but he's one weird fish himself. Or just rude. Either way, I have no intention of making any more effort with him. I've tried twice now and he's just too cool for school. Why would I bother with him when there are lovely people like Margot, Paige, and Leo to chat to? He can sod off.'

'I'm not rude or weird...' She turned quickly to find the man standing a few feet from her front porch and he had clearly heard every word. 'And I'm definitely not cool. I don't think I've ever been cool.' He scratched under his cap with his free hand. 'Apart from maybe one night in 1986 when I borrowed my dad's car to impress a girl. It was a balmy night; Van Halen was on the radio...' He paused, as if this was one detail too many. 'I'm just not used to talking to folks. I keep myself to myself.'

'Gosh! I... I didn't mean...' She stopped rubbing her foot and stared at him, now cap free, as embarrassment snaked over her.

'I brought you a couple of these.' He held out two of the beautiful brown fish. 'You can throw them on the grill with a squeeze of lemon, a little bit of garlic, and a brush of oil. Alls you need is some good bread and a gulp of cold beer and it's the best meal you'll get this side of Linden Falls.'

'I'm a chef actually!' She didn't know why she blurted this, but it felt good to hear his recipe, his enthusiasm for simple food and flavours, a connection of sorts.

'Ah, so you don't need me to tell you how to cook the things.' He took a step forward and she accepted the gift from his tanned hands, noting his busted fingernails, a man who worked outside if she had to guess.

'I take it you like to cook too? Your eyes lit up when you mentioned the cooking of the fish...'

'Not really.' He looked sideways and gave a small laugh. 'But I've cooked in some odd places with few ingredients, so I guess I know how to make the best of simple things.' He met her eye line. 'I'm a vet.'

'Oh! Well, how marvellous!' She clapped, feeling a slight shame at how she had misjudged the man and his career. 'I love animals too. We used to have a dog called Tilly when I was growing up, a chocolate Lab, but she passed away. Still one of the saddest days of my life! Mummy cried for a month. And then living just off the Kings Road, SW3 didn't really allow for dog life. I was too busy in the restaurant. But I have Wordsworth. He's a cat. Don't know how you do it! All that emotion and the terrible conversations when an animal is not going to make it. It must be so hard?'

'I have no idea what you just said.' He stared at her.

Verity laughed out loud. 'Oh, that's funny! Is it my accent or because I speak too quickly?'

'Yes.' His reply.

She laughed again and he joined in. He looked very different when he relaxed, handsome even. His eyes crinkled and his mouth opened a little. He was, if she had to guess, late fifties, and was in good shape. Must be the handling of all those animals keeping him fit.

'I'm not a veterinary but a vet—an army vet. I was in the military.'

Verity felt the smile slip from her face. 'Oh, my goodness. I'm so embarrassed right now.' She closed her eyes and tried to hide as much of her face as she could with her hand.

'Don't be. What's the phrase? *America and England, two nations separated by a common language?* Or something like that.' He kicked at the dirt floor with the toe of his work boot.

'Yes, something like that.' The two held each other's gaze for a moment, making a connection of sorts, starting over almost. 'So you're no longer in the military?'

'No.' He wiped his mouth, and she heard the rough skin of his hand graze the bristle of his unshaven lip. 'Now I paint.'

'On canvas or houses and fences?' She didn't want to make any more assumptions.

'Canvas. I'm an artist, I guess.' He kept his eyes down and looked a little embarrassed, suggesting this new career was still something that he was growing accustomed to voicing, as if the creative skin was taking a little while to adhere to the bones of the military man. 'I sell at galleries in Ithaca and other places in Upstate New York.'

'What do you paint?' She was curious.

'Nature, fish. Water, trees, the sky...' He shrugged. 'I spend the summer here, fishing and painting, and in the winter head farther up into the Green Mountains, where I still paint, but it's a different palette and I get to ski and enjoy the quiet, the snow. I like it.'

'Cold though?'

'Yes, snow tends to be that way.'

She smiled, liking his subtle sarcasm. 'Well, I'd like to see your paintings. If you have any or want to show me, I mean. I wasn't inviting myself or anything.' Again she garbled.

'Sure.' He gave a small nod and turned to leave without making any arrangement or giving any indication that he would like her to see his work.

'What was the song, the Van Halen song that made you cool?' she called out.

'"Why Can't This be Love?" you know it?' he shouted over his shoulder but kept on walking.

'Yes, we have Van Halen in London too!'

He nodded.

She watched him lope off down the track and studied the fish in her hand.

'What an odd chap,' she surmised, but the flare of attraction in the base of her gut was unmistakable, no matter how odd.

With a restorative cup of tea in her palm and having gorged on the truffled mac and cheese, Verity sat in the chair opposite her daughter.

'You mustn't ever feel pulled, Soph. I really don't want that.'

'What d'you mean?' She looked up from her novel, putting her finger on the page to hold her place.

'I mean that things might take a bit of getting used to for me with Dad and Freya, and there may be moments of awkwardness while we all navigate this new life, but you should never feel conflicted. You love us both and that's wonderful, but I'd hate you to feel that you had to hide your thoughts, feelings, or plans from either of us. You need to just keep being you, okay?'

'Okay.' Sophie turned back to her book and Verity thought it a rather inadequate answer to the point she was making. Clearly the world of vampires and rainy small-town America was more gripping than anything she might have to say.


IT WAS A WEEK LATER, midafternoon, that Sophie ambushed her as she walked through the door with two brown bags full of groceries. Her mouth watered at the thought of the fat Brie, crisp rye crackers, and fancy apple chutney that she had picked up from the deli.

'Is it okay if you take me back into town later, Mum?'

'Oh, really, Sophie! First, I've only just got back; second, I've told you that hunting down an internet signal is not what this trip is about. You need to immerse yourself in the experience, read your book! Walk the trails! Chop a log.'

'Chop a log?' Her daughter pulled a face.

'Well, obviously not! I wouldn't let you handle an axe. Far too dangerous. But you get my gist.' She shoved the bags onto the countertop.

'I do. And for your information, I wasn't going back into town to seek out an internet signal but to meet someone.'

'Meet someone?' This had her attention. 'Who are you meeting? You've only been here five minutes?'

'His name is Roland Pickard, and he writes poetry.'

She didn't know whether to laugh or cry, delighted Sophie had made a friend but instantly suspicious that Roland Pickard might be a slick, silver-tongued seducer who knew that the way to grab the interest of a girl like Sophie was to whip out a poetry book and whisper it seductively!

'Where did you meet Roland?'

'By the Wishing Tree, on our first day. We swapped numbers and now we text.'

Verity smiled. *Now we text...* as if that was a stage in courtship. Maybe it was. She was sorely out of practice.

'Ah, the famous Wishing Tree!' She rolled her eyes to show her dismissal of the concept. 'And how old is he?'

'Twenty.'

'*Twenty?*' she screeched with a rising sense of panic. 'That's much older than you!' She pointed out the obvious without pointing out the obvious.

'Three years, Mum! There's seven between you and Dad!'

'That's different.'

'Why is it?' Sophie stared at her.

*Because twenty-year-old boys want to have sex. Twenty-year-old boys know the world more than you do. Twenty-year-old boys can be intoxicating and full of promise... when you are seventeen. And a twenty-year-old boy might hurt your heart... and that's not something I can condone. Not on this trip!*

'Because you will have had different life experiences.' She put it as succinctly as she could.

'But you want me to have different life experiences! That's exactly what you said! One minute you're telling me to go and chop logs and the next you're telling me not to try anything different!'

'Knock knock!' Leo stood on the step and called through the open door.

'Hey, Leo. Come in!'

'Is this a bad time?' Their host hung back, having obviously picked up on a little of their conversation or at least heard their raised voices.

'No! Not at all. Sophie and I were just about to have a row.'

'Oh, should I come back later?' She pointed with her thumb back down the track.

'No, it won't take long.' Verity pulled a fake wide

smile. 'I'm just explaining to my daughter why it might not be a good idea to meet up with a twenty-year-old boy she doesn't know and that his intentions might not be strictly… honourable.'

'Wow! That's a lot.'

'Tell me about it.' Sophie sighed. 'It is a lot.'

'Who's the boy?' Leo asked casually.

'Roland Pickard,' Sophie answered and folded her arms tightly across her chest.

Leo gave a broad smile. 'Well, it's not my place to offer advice or guidance on a family matter, and Lord knows I don't want to interfere, but I can vouch for Roland Pickard. Known him since before he was born. His parents go to my church. He's a math genius, book-ish, and if I had to draw up a list of all the boys in Linden Falls, in fact the whole of Vermont, whose intentions would be "honourable," Roland would prob-ably be at the very top, or second top after Pastor Quinn.' She paused and looked upward. 'In fact he'd come before Pastor Quinn, just remembered an inci-dent a while back at the church picnic. Anyhoo, wondered if you fancied some company? Just checking in. Margot said you were a little down when she saw you last week.'

'Oh, Leo, that's so kind.' She felt reassured, not only by Leo's description of the boy but also her visit and the fact that Margot had cared enough to comment. 'Why don't I run Sophie in to meet her bookish mathematician and we can get together when I come back?'

'Roland said he'd run me home later. He comes right past here,' Sophie added.

'Yes, they live up the valley a little way,' Leo confirmed. 'I'll grab some of Walt's homemade wine and we can sit on the deck. How about that?'

'Sounds perfect.' She meant it; the prospect of socializing and drinking Walt's homemade wine sounded good. 'I have Brie!'

'Good for you!' Leo clicked her tongue inside her mouth as she headed off to grab wine.


VERITY ACCEPTED the kiss on her cheek from her daughter and watched as she sauntered across the town square and past the darn Wishing Tree. Her wish was that she hadn't been so daft and tied her thoughts onto one of its branches. Sophie's words still danced in her thoughts. *Dad's face... he looks like there's nowhere else he would rather be... He wants to take me to St. Lucia for Christmas...*

'You are right, little Soph, we weren't that happy when we were together. I need to find a way to let go,' she whispered into the air, as a tall, gangly boy with dark, thick-framed glasses rose from a bench to greet her child. Verity smiled. He looked nervous, his movements and stance sweet, and she could see in an instant that Leo was right—the kid did not look like a silver-tongued seducer. It was with relief that she turned the car around, off to find solace with her new friend, a chunk of good cheese, and a bottle of homemade wine.

. . .

THERE WAS something about sitting on the wooden step with a glass of plonk as the sun slowly set that drew any lingering stress from her muscles. Here in Linden Falls, it was as if the world turned at a different pace, one that allowed her to breathe, to think.

Leo raised the bottle. 'Drop more?'

'Oh, God no! This has gone straight to my head!' she exhaled.

'Mine too. Walt's wine sure packs a punch.' Leo laughed, her rosy cheeks and cackle suggesting that no matter how long she had been sampling her husband's home brew, she was not immune to its effects.

'What's in this?' Verity studied the slightly cloudy concoction, as if she might see a clue. Her head swam, and her vision was a little fuzzy. 'I think I'm a little drunk.'

'You know, honey, a little bit of drunk can sometimes be just what the doctor ordered.'

'Well, I like the sound of that doctor! And actually, Leo, I'm not a little bit drunk, I think I might be a whole lot drunk.'

'I can see that.' Her tone was kindly. She had in such a short time smudged the lines of formality. Verity considered her a friend.

'Oh no!' She put her hand over her face and made a deep wailing sound.

'What's the matter?' Leo sat forward and palmed circles on her back; it was both motherly and kind.

'I'm going to cry. I can feel it,' she sniffed, in the first stages of emotion and a hint as to what was to follow. After putting her wineglass down, she flapped her hands in front of her face. 'This is what happens. I have all these feelings and this upset swirling inside me, and I manage to keep it all in and can even rationalize things, but alcohol is like the correct code to punch in and let it all out! It opens the door!'

'That's okay, honey, sometimes it's okay to open that door.'

'I don't want to open the dooooooor!' Verity let her head fall onto her chest. 'I don't want to think about it. I'm supposed to be learning to thrive! But the fact is Sonny left me. He left me for Freya bloody Walsh, and she is young, Leo! I secretly look at pictures of her on my phone. She wears very red lipstick, and she looks good in it! She's young. Did I mention that? And pert and funny, and I bet she doesn't have a leaky bladder when she laughs, and I bet she takes the time to shave her legs and probably wears slinky knickers. My knickers are grey and baggy, and I only shave my shins in the summer. I gave up...'

'So'—Leo sat up straight, her tone calm and strong —'you think your husband walked out on your marriage because of the state of your underwear and a few hairs on your shin?'

Verity nodded; her bottom lip stuck out like a toddler. 'I do a bit. I mean, I know there was more to it, but I could have tried more... I was always so tired, and—'

'Let me stop you right there, missy!' The older woman held up her hand as if addressing a toddler. 'You need to cut out that kind of talk. You were tired because you were working hard for your business; you were tired because you were running a home, being a parent, organising everyone's lives, and he ducked out and went elsewhere to Miss Slinky Knickers because he's a shit and not because you didn't shave your legs! Don't forget that.'

Verity felt the bubble of laughter. 'Miss Slinky Knickers!' Her friend was right, of course; this misplaced guilt and self-recrimination were as pointless as they were inaccurate. *Sonny was a shit! I mean, yes, a great dad, an outstanding chef, but still a shit!* She had held him in such high esteem for so long, certainly influenced by the way their staff, the media, and the fee-paying customers treated him, as if he was some kind of alchemist and not simply a hardworking, big-egoed man who knew how to dot a tasty foam on a perfectly seared scallop!

'The truth is'—she drew her knees up and rested her arms on them as she looked out over the valley and the ridgeline that fell away from the farm in sharp angles—'he's right, we'd become more like associates, colleagues, co-parents, but we weren't lovers. We weren't even great friends, not recently. Both in our own little busy bubbles, getting through the day,'

'It happens.' Leo's succinct appraisal.

'It does, and so why does it hurt so much? Why is it that, even when I can see that we had crumbled and that neither of us was truly happy, why am I in mourning?'

'Because he's your husband. Because you have history. Because maybe you didn't question your future. Because it's a shock. Because change is alarming. Because you're scared. Because you're jealous... Take your pick.'

Verity nodded. 'You're right. Yes, to all of them. And it feels like we've let Sophie down.' This confession enough to summon a fresh batch of tears.

'You haven't. It's just life. And from what I've seen, she's a great kid and you're doing a great job, and the fact that you're worried enough to give a damn about how this all affects her means you're already halfway there. Marriages break down all the time. Life throws rocks at us and it's how we learn to dodge them that strengthens us, Sophie included.'

Verity took a long, slow breath. Her head was clearing a little and she felt the first pull of sleep. 'I said something similar to her earlier and I think you're right. I am scared. This is the first time in my life that I don't know what comes next.' She looked up at the stars shining brightly overhead in the inky blue canopy of night, as if this might be where the answer lay. 'My life has always followed a predictable trajectory, and yet here I am, forty-six, without the first clue as to what comes next.'

'I get it, but it doesn't have to be scary, it can be exciting! You just have to reframe your thoughts. It's not the end, it's a beginning! You haven't been dumped, you've been set free!'

'So why do I feel so lost?'

'You won't always. Trust me. Walt got diagnosed with Parkinson's a few years back and I didn't know which way was up, but we figured it out. Things settle and it gets easier. It becomes your normal.'

'I'm sorry to hear that about Walt.'

'He's good; we're happy.' Her friend smiled as she had a habit of doing when she mentioned her husband. 'It's just a bump in the road, but we carry on...'

'Oh no, Leo! I think I might be sick.' Verity closed her eyes and took deep breaths.

'Okaaay, well, let's get you to bed. Walt'll be wondering where I've got to.'

'It's hard, isn't it?'

'What?' Leo wrinkled her nose like she had lost the thread.

'Life! Everything! Oh no, here we go!' Verity jumped up and ran into the trees, where she promptly vomited. Bending over and holding her hair in one hand, she looked back at her new friend. 'I've been sick on my shoes!'

'Mum? What are you doing?' She hadn't heard Sophie return or approach. 'Are you being sick? Are you okay?'

Guilt flushed sobriety through her veins. How awful for her child to see her semi-inebriated and with sick on her pumps.

'I'm being a bit sick.' She righted herself and tried to

keep her words sharp as she swayed. 'I think I might've had something that didn't wholly agree with me.' She kept her gaze low and wiped her mouth.

'Ah, yes, I remember when Dad did the same on New Year's. A bottle of bad bacon...' Sophie smiled and folded her arms across her chest, looking far older and wiser than her seventeen years.

It hurt to recall that golden night, spent in front of the fire with board games, red wine, and generous glasses of port that had resulted in Sonny being more than a little hungover. He had announced, when he joined her and Sophie at the breakfast table the next morning, that his malaise was probably down to some dodgy bacon he had snaffled as a snack en route to bed, and Sophie had quipped, 'I suspect a whole bottle of bad bacon...' and they had howled their laughter at her insight and wit. He had looked sheepish, embarrassed, and Verity had made him tea, pouring just enough love into the cup to keep the icy chill of sickness from his bones. The memory was enough to summon her tears again.

She nodded and laughed through them. 'Yes, darling, that was it, a bottle of bad bacon.'

'Come on, Mum. Let's get you to bed.'

Verity nodded and took her daughter's hand, as Leo gathered the empty bottle and waved her goodbye.

'How was poetry and math boy?' Verity asked as she pulled the patchwork quilt over her legs and sank into the soft mattress of her bed.

AMANDA PROWSE

'Nice. Smart. I like him. I mean, just as friends, but I like him.'

'Friends are good.' She smiled as her eyelids grew heavy. 'Have you spoken to Paloma, Eliza, and Darius?'

Sophie paused in the doorway. 'The girls, yes, Darius, no. He hasn't answered my calls or returned my texts.'

'Are you upset about that?' She leaned up on her elbow and the room spun a little.

'I was talking to Roland about it, and he said that Darius sounded like the kind of guy who was interested when there was free food at the restaurant or Dad got tickets for an event, but he didn't sound like a "no matter what" friend. You know, one of those people who just loves you for you and nothing else matters.'

'Leo said he was smart.' She laid her head on the soft pillow and felt the pull of sleep.

'I'm not going to bother contacting Darius again.'

'Out of sight, out of mind is not what you deserve, Soph. You want someone to want you, to miss you, to see you...'

'I do.' Her smart girl nodded assuredly. 'I do. Night night, sleep tight, don't let the bugs bite!'

Sophie closed the door quietly, and Verity smiled at the role reversal. Her last thought before falling asleep was that Leo was not only right about Roland but also that she had to reframe her thoughts. This was a beginning... and she would start by washing her pumps, getting new knickers, and shaving her legs.

# CHAPTER 3

'What can I get you?' Moira, the friendly waitress at Doc's, greeted her a little too loudly for comfort, not that she was loud, but today, Verity's hearing was rather sensitive. The anvil of a headache struck inside her skull. Even running the tap to clean her teeth was a cacophony, which made her wince.

'Coffee. Lots of coffee, please. A bucket full of coffee or intravenous coffee, is that a thing?'

'Leave it with me.' Moira spoke softly now and got busy with the fancy machine.

Verity patted the counter like it was an old friend and took a seat at a table with a direct view of the square.

'Thought it was you! I'm Cassie. I run Bistro Claudine. Leo told me you were in town, and I just nipped in to have a word with you, Verity.'

Verity removed her sunglasses, which had helped a

little with the morning glare. This was quite standard in Linden Falls, the old-world friendliness and charm that were both warm and welcoming.

Cassie narrowed her eyes in concern. 'Are you okay?' She clearly had a big heart and her concern, no matter how touching, was both misplaced and embarrassing. How was she to explain that she might be a grown-ass woman but had misjudged her alcohol intake and was suffering the after effects? 'Is it hay fever, do you think?' Cassie probed.

'Possibly.' She gave a small smile. 'Yes, it might be.'

'Ouch and what with you reeling from Walt's home brew, hay fever is the last thing you need, right?' Cassie laughed.

'That was mean. But funny. Sit down!' Liking the woman on sight, she moved her bag from the chair next to her.

'I can't.' Cassie pointed toward the door. 'I'm running errands, but I'm glad I caught you. A little bird tells me you are not just a chef but an outstanding, award-winning, Michelin-starred chef. Is it true?' Her eyes were wide and bright.

'Well, they were awarded to my husband and the restaurant we run, but I am part of the brigade.' What else to say? *It's been my life for years, prepping food, cooking food, tasting food, creating menus, thinking about food every waking minute...*

'So how about you come and guest chef for me at Claudine's? We could run a special evening—you'd have full control over the menu, the kitchen, whatever you need. It'd be so great for us and a good way for you to meet everyone. What do you think?' Cassie's smile was too wide for Verity to give a no outright

'I think I'll think about it. I'm supposed to be on holiday!' She chuckled but had to admit the idea of getting back into a kitchen filled her with a certain joy.

'Okay then, gotta dash, but let me know!' Cassie clapped her hands with a look of excited anticipation, as if Verity had already said yes. 'Oh, and I sure hope your hay fever clears up soon.' She left with a wink.

Verity smiled and caught sight of Sophie sitting on the grass by the Wishing Tree, throwing her head back and laughing at something Roland had said. Deciding fresh air might be just the thing to clear her head, she thanked Moira, grabbed her coffee to go, and meandered out in the sunshine.

'Hey, Soph!' she called as she approached. The boy jumped up from the bench and ran his palm down the front of his shirt as if smartening up. It was a sweet and endearing gesture.

'You must be Roland.'

'Yes, ma'am.' He nodded and held her eye line. His was an open, honest face and she liked him on sight.

'And I hear you are a bit of a mathematician? My math is appalling. So, if I can't find the calculator app on my phone, I'm stuck!'

'He's a great poet too, Mum!' Sophie championed her new friend.

'I think it's rare to be good with numbers and words. You must be super smart.'

Roland pushed his glasses back onto the bridge of his nose from where they had slipped. His face blushed at the compliment, and his shy smile hinted at delight. 'I think the two are similar. Math is no more than a formula, a pattern, and poetry too, whether it's haiku, seventeen syllables in three lines of five, seven, five, or iambic pentameter, a beat, a rhythm, as I say, a formula...'

'I guess so.' She felt a little overawed by his smarts. 'You should come up to see us sometime, Roland. I make a mean steak.'

'I would like that, but I'm actually vegan,' he offered a little apologetically.

'Well, that's easy then.' She tapped her bottom lip. 'I'm thinking roasted cauliflower steak with dukkah and crushed hazelnuts, a fennel purée and baby charred leeks, served on spiced apricot couscous, with a pomegranate molasses glaze. How does that sound?'

Now she was in her comfort zone—food was the subject in which she was most confident and spoke without thinking ahead as to whether she could easily get all the ingredients in Linden Falls.

'It sounds amazing!'

His face lit up and Sophie seemed a little delighted at the prospect. Verity noticed that she hadn't mentioned Darius for a while. She couldn't deny the fact that she considered it to be no bad thing. A car honked its horn loudly. Verity spun around, in time to see Jack Darby pulling up into a parking space in front of the inn. Neva Cabot was crossing the road and jumped at the sound that cracked the air. Jack waved by way of apology.

'It's my mum's cowboy.' Sophie pulled a face at Roland, who laughed, and Verity felt her face colour.

'He is certainly not my cowboy. In that he's not a cowboy and he's certainly not mine!' she rebuked, a little embarrassed by the whole conversation and aware of how her heart and spirit lifted a little at the sight of him. With the coffee doing its job and the fresh air on her skin, all lingering traces of her hangover were forgotten.

Jack slowly climbed down from his truck, and she noted the curve of his back muscles inside his short-sleeve tee before looking away. Walking leisurely, he came over and raised his hand.

'Hey.'

'Hi, Jack!' She disliked the slight warble to her voice as nerves bit, wishing she could do it over and sound a little cooler, cool like borrowing your dad's car with Van Halen playing on a balmy night...

'Thought it was you.' He rested his thumbs in his belt loops and said nothing else, as if it was obvious that he would stop and come over.

'We were just talking poetry,' Sophie threw into the mix.

'Well, goodbye then!' Jack turned to walk away, and Roland laughed. It broke the tension. 'Only poetry I know is learned from the men's locker room and is not for sharing in polite company.'

'Me too,' Verity added and it was Jack's turn to laugh.

'You ever wish on the tree, Mr Darby?' Sophie asked as they all turned to look at the display of ribbons and messages blowing gently in the breeze.

'Nope.'

'So, you don't believe in the magic?' Verity stared at him, her mouth twitching into a smile.

'I think it's probably a load of old baloney, but if folks get something out of it, then who am I to judge?'

'We're going to the bookshop to see Gladys.' Sophie hitched her bag over her shoulder and she and Roland fell into step. 'See you later, Mum, Mr Darby.'

'Well, thanks for the invite!' Verity called to the back of the giggling twosome, who sped up as they walked away from her. 'I'd like to see the dog too!'

'Actually, I was coming over to *invite* you fishing, if you'd like?'

'What? Right now?' She bit her lip, having never been fishing, unsure if she'd like it at all.

'Yes, right now. Truck's loaded and I have sandwiches.'

'What kind of sandwiches? This could be a deal breaker,' she half joked.

'Tuna.'

'Tuna! You can't eat tuna while you're fishing! That's just cruel!' she yelped.

'It's okay, I tell the fish they're cheese.' He smiled.

She liked his humour and the fact that it felt like

they had broken down a barrier. 'If I don't like fishing, can you drop me back at my car?'

'Sure. Although I can't understand why anyone on God's green earth wouldn't like fishing.' He shrugged and she followed him to his truck, where fishing kit and sandwiches awaited. She tripped after him with a spring in her step and a lacing of joy around her spirit.

'NOTHING! I can't believe we sat there for three whole hours and didn't get so much as a sniff! We could have just stopped at the market and bought fish! It would have been a whole lot quicker.' She kicked the deck outside her room, where they now sat on the worn rocking chairs, watching dusk pull its blind on the day.

'Where would the fun be in that?'

'Well, we'd have fish!' She giggled.

'I guess on the plus side, what with no catch, you got to eat your tuna sandwich without feeling guilty. And mine too.' He had peered into the empty lunchbox, as if hoping that if he stared enough, another sandwich might appear.

'I honestly hadn't realised I was that hungry! At home I eat a big meal late morning, we all sit down together in the restaurant before we open for lunch service, and that kind of does me, sees me through my shifts, and then if I fancy a snack, it's just cheese and bits and bobs from the fridge when I get home, but here'—she breathed long and slow—'Sophie and I are eating differently, not so many big meals, a lunch of fruit and yoghurt, all good stuff, but I think today my body needed carbs.'

'Apparently so.' He smiled and took a swig of his beer from the bottle. 'I can't imagine the life you lead. Heck I can't picture what you are talking about a lot of the time.'

She tilted her head and looked at his profile, a good, strong nose and those kind crinkles around his very blue eyes. 'There's a lot about my life that I love: my friends, my family of course, the architecture, and the buzz of life in the capital city. Like Samuel Johnson said, "If you're tired of London then you're tired of life," and I was tired, that's for sure. It's a faster life, a noisy life. A bit like being on a hamster wheel and not knowing how to step off. That's the truth.'

'Seems like the wilds of Vermont are exactly what you need, especially with a deck like this.' He had already commented that she had a premium view and that he would be complaining to Leo at the earliest opportunity. 'What made you come here over everywhere else on the planet?'

'Ah, now, that's a funny old story. Would you believe me if I said I closed my eyes and stuck my fingers on the globe, and this was where they landed?'

'Nope.'

'No, me either and yet that's what happened. It felt like a joke at first and yet here we are!'

'Here we are.' He turned to face her. 'I've liked spending time with you today.'

'I've liked spending time with you. Thank you for stopping to pick me up.' She drew breath and asked the question that had been bothering her all afternoon. 'Do you take many women fishing, Jack? Is this what you do? Entice them in with your indifferent attitude, then take them fishing, hoping they bite?'

'The fish or the women?' he quipped.

'Both.' She was serious.

Jack sat forward in the chair. 'Actually, you're the first person I've taken fishing in all the time I've been here. I'm very picky about who I spend my time with.'

'In that case, I'm honoured.' She meant it. Her heart beat a little faster, partly with sheer joy at his revelation, but also in fear of what she had to say next. 'I just want to say, Jack, that, I'm... I'm rather damaged goods.' She spoke steadily and quietly.

He gave a half laugh. 'Is that right?'

'Uh-huh.' She felt small, self-conscious.

'You think you're the only one? You think a place as pretty as Linden Falls isn't crammed with folks just trying to get by? Don't be fooled by a hanging basket, a picket fence, a painted sign, and a cheery greeting. Everyone is doing what they need to do, and some wear their troubles well or hide them altogether and others not so much.'

'I guess so.'

'Believe it!' He shifted in the chair.

'I'm still getting used to the way things are now. It's not so much that I miss my husband as miss someone. I liked being in a pair. Like matching socks or fancy mittens. It made me feel comfortable. Do you know what I mean?'

'I do.' He shifted on the seat.

'Do you ever get lonely up here, Jack?'

'Sometimes, but I kind of like my own company. Spent too many years in bunks with snoring soldiers, so now I like the peace of nighttime in particular.'

'But marriage can be so cosy, comforting... when it goes right.'

'Yes.' He shifted on the seat. 'Although it's been a while for me.'

'You were married? Sorry, I shouldn't pry, but Leo said...' She stopped talking, not wanting him to think they had been gossiping or that he had been the topic of that gossip, both of which were true.

'I was married for ten years, been divorced about the same. She was a nice lady. Is a nice lady. I liked her, but'—he took his time—'sometimes nice is not enough. Sometimes you gotta like yourself before you can start to love another.'

'Why didn't you like yourself?' She pulled the question from the ashes of his statement.

'I guess the life I led, the job I did, the company I kept. Afghanistan was no vacation. I lost good friends, and some of those who came home were changed.'

'Were you changed, Jack?' she whispered, hardly daring to ask, feeling drawn to the man who had such presence and unsure whether this was too personal a question for two such newly acquainted.

He took his time. 'Physically, no. Mentally, hell

yeah! I felt, *feel* a lot of guilt about those who didn't come home. Therapy has helped me understand that I need to learn to live with the new version of myself, and now I feel like I need to live for myself and for all those who fought for that very freedom.'

'I can't imagine what it must have been like.' She felt a wave of sadness at the picture his words conjured.

'I'm sure glad you can't.' His words were offered without sarcasm, and they touched her.

'And are you'—the words were not easily found— 'are you better now?' She winced at her clumsy expression of a concern that was heartfelt.

Jack nodded. 'Getting there. Day by day. I'm very different to the man who set off in new boots and with high hopes, but I figure that's okay. I did what I needed to do, and I did what I could.'

'That's all anyone can ever ask, isn't it?'

'Yes, ma'am.'

'It sounds so funny when anyone calls me ma'am; it makes me think of a head teacher or royalty! When in reality I am a slightly batty chef who is on the run.'

'A very clever chef, according to Cassie, who told me she was going to try and get you to cook in the bistro one evening.'

'Oh, I think she was just being kind.' Verity took the compliment and swallowed it whole, loving the taste of it. 'I don't feel very clever. In fact, quite the opposite. I feel…' She hesitated.

'You feel what?' He turned to face her. She studied

the long eyelashes that framed his eyes. Pretty lashes for a man.

'Stupid. My husband has made me feel stupid.' It was the first time she had voiced this. It felt both exposing and cathartic. 'Not that he'll be my husband for much longer, I guess, and then what do I call him, my ex? Sophie's dad? I haven't given that any thought. But it'll be odd to have that official level of separation.'

He shrugged, as he was wont to do.

'I'm wittering. I do that when I'm nervous.'

'And you're nervous now?' He kept his eyes on his boots, his legs stretched out in front of him.

'A little. I haven't had many people to talk to like this, although I did get a little tipsy and spill my guts to Leo last night.'

'Yes, I might have heard about that.'

'Jeez, does everyone know everything around here?' She covered her face with her hands.

'Pretty much. Welcome to small-town life.' He grinned.

'I try to keep a smile on for Sophie, but it can all feel a little overwhelming at times. Like it's unreal. I'm here and it's just the most perfect place, but then I remember the shit storm that's waiting for me in London.'

Jack scratched at his stubbled beard. 'It's a whole other world, that's for sure.'

There was a beat of silence that was far from uncomfortable.

'And for the record'—he took a long, slow breath—'I

think it's your husband who is stupid. Seems like he didn't know when he had it good.'

She smiled at the compliment and folded her hands in her lap. 'Just not good enough, apparently. And I know it sounds crass, but it wouldn't be so bad if he had just up and left or told me we were through. I think what hurts the most is that he's cast me aside for a younger, prettier version. I can't compete, and I didn't know I had to.'

'You got a picture? I'd sure like to see her!' He chuckled, and she couldn't help but follow suit.

'God! Listen to me! I know I sound desperate but it's the truth. I wanted to be enough. I always wanted to be enough and the fact that I'm not...'

'Ever thought that you might be looking at it wrong? Maybe it's not that you weren't enough but that you were too much? 'Cause I reckon you'd be enough for any right-thinking man.'

His words and sentiments echoed Leo's, and she felt the rise of a blush on her chest and was sure that he too could hear her heart beating.

'You say the nicest things to me, Jack.'

'They're not just words, Verty, they're what I'm thinking, and I haven't thought that way for the longest time.'

Swallowing, she felt the leap of desire in her gut, a feeling that had been absent in her life for longer than she could recall. Her fingers twitched with the need to touch his skin, and as she leaned closer to the man who had filled her thoughts, she inhaled the scent of him, woody and peppery, but with the floral notes of his sweet cologne. After putting his beer bottle down on the step, Jack reached out and ran the calloused pad of his thumb along her jawline. It sent a shiver through her limbs that felt a lot like an awakening. Turning her head toward him, Verity closed her eyes and waited to feel the touch of his lips against her own, waited to kiss a man who was not her husband, for the first time in decades. She held her breath, her fingertips rested on his strong forearm, and her toes curled in her espadrilles. She wanted badly for him to kiss her. Her, frumpy old Verity Joseph, the forty-six-year-old abandoned wife of superstar chef Sonny, felt nothing but longing for this handsome man who held her in his thrall.

'Mum!'

'Oh, Lord!' Verity shot backwards as if Sophie's shout had hit her physically. Jumping up, she tucked her shirt into her jeans and ran from the rear deck, through the house, and out onto the front porch, where Roland and Sophie jumped out of his open-topped Jeep.

'Soph! Gosh! Hello!' She was flustered. 'I didn't think you'd be back till morning. What a lovely surprise! Come in.'

'What do you mean come in? Why are you being so weird? Of course I'm going to come in. I live here too! And we're not staying. I've only nipped back to fetch my swimsuit. I forgot it and everyone's going to jump in the lake. This is practically on the way.'

'Of course, yes!' Sophie dashed past her. 'How... how are you, Roland?' She tried to still her racing pulse, feeling like a teenage whose parents had arrived home sooner than expected and caught her fooling around on the couch.

'Good, thank you, Mrs Joseph.'

'Good. Good.' Verity marvelled at how a second felt like a minute, as she rocked on her heels and folded her arms, as she and the boy stared awkwardly and silently down the lane. She willed her daughter to hurry. Not only was the silence deafening, but she was more than a little keen to get back to Jack and pick up where they had left off. She was, however, equally keen for Sophie to leave without knowing he was there at all, worrying that it all might be a little too soon for her girl, who had a lot to deal with already. Her parents splitting up and feeling left behind by her friends, for starters.

Sophie hurtled through the front door with her swimsuit and a towel bundled under her arm. 'Now you sure you won't be lonely, Mum?'

'I won't, darling. Don't you worry about me. A cup of cocoa and a quick chapter of my novel and I will be in the land of nod. Just have a lovely time!'

'I feel really bad leaving you on your own.' Sophie pulled a sad face and called out, as she clambered back into the Jeep and Roland took his place at the wheel.

'Don't! I'll be fine! I like my own company.' She added cheerily, 'And you've got your key?'

'I have.' Sophie patted her pocket.

'Drive carefully, Roland,' she called.

'Always, Mrs Joseph.'

'Well, if you're sure you're going to be okay?' her daughter beamed at her.

'I am. Thank you, sweet girl. I shall see you in the morning. Don't let the bugs bite!' Verity waved even though they were yet to leave.

'Oh, and Mum?' Sophie called as Roland revved the engine, ready to leave.

'Yes, darling?'

'We've just seen Mr Darby scuttling through the undergrowth, as if escaping, but he's left his hat on the table. Make sure he gets it, won't you?' This was her girl's parting shot as the little car sped off, kicking up dust as it went.

'I...' Verity wasn't often lost for words.

Closing the front door, she drew the latch and paused to look at her reflection in the mirror that hung on the wall. Her skin held the rosy glow of joy and her eyes had lost the bruises of fatigue that had been camping at the tops of her cheekbones. She smiled and for once her thoughts were not of Sonny or sweet revenge or how she wished he could see the moment and feel nothing but envy... No, in fact, she was jolly glad he could not see her right now. The girl he had swept up the aisle with so many promises, the girl now a woman who might just have been too much for him.

'Maybe you are right, Jack. Maybe I am too bloody fabulous!' she whispered as she went to gather her neighbour's hat, which would need returning in the morning, glad of the excuse to go and visit him.

※》

THE NEW DAY began with sunlight filtering through the open French doors. The air was still, and Verity leapt out of bed, hoping to catch Jack before he headed off for a day of paintin' and fishin'. She threw on her cutoffs, an old tee, and her worn sandals, filled with nothing but the warm glow of happiness. Birdsong was her wake-up call. Taking a minute, she stood on the track with her arms outstretched and let the sun bathe her face as something that felt a lot like hope flooded her being.

'Morning!' she yelled, spying him on his front step.

'Morning. A couple of minutes earlier and you'd have caught me dancing. It's nice to dance in the sunlight, makes you feel good.' He turned his face to the sky and held his arms up above his head.

'Oh, very funny!' She plumped down next to him. 'You forgot your hat.' She placed it on his head, and he caught her wrist before bringing it up to his mouth and gently kissing the palm of her hand. It caused the breath to stop in her throat.

'You're a surprise.' His voice croaked.

She leaned closer to him. 'In what way a surprise?'

He took a deep breath. 'I guess I wasn't looking to meet anyone, so that was a surprise. And I never thought I'd meet a fast-talking Brit and feel this way. That's a big surprise, but the biggest is how you seem to make everything else disappear.' He knitted her fingers with his. Her hand looked small as he held it close to his throat.

'What... what do you mean?' Her words came from a mouth sticky with nerves.

'I mean that when I sit next to you or drink coffee with you or watch you laugh, all the bad stuff goes away, just fades into the distance, like it never happened or just isn't important. I only see you.'

'I only see you.' She echoed the sentiment, remembering Sophie's words and knowing that, finally, she was beginning to like the view, excited to look out over the possibilities of a new and different life.

He kissed her then, tenderly and with none of the passion that could often be a forerunner to sex, but with gentleness that spoke of friendship and with a promise of longevity, the kiss of a partner and not just a lover. It fired bolts of fear and joy through her very core. She didn't want her body to make promises that her mind could not keep.

'I don't know what happens next, Verty. I don't know how much time we have,'

'How much time do you want?' It felt audacious and at the same time necessary to ask.

'All of it.' He paused. 'Right now I want all the time we have left while you are here in Linden Falls.'

She closed her eyes and felt his arm about her shoulders. The glow of joy she felt at his admission was, however, spiked through with thoughts that London waited for her—the house, the business, even Wordsworth the fat cat, who Mrs Roper, their neighbour, liked to feed. She blinked away the reality of what lay ahead and inhaled the scent of his skin, wanting to commit every small aspect of him to memory for the days when the rain fell and she was far away and the sky was grey, knowing she would drift to this moment of happiness, because that was how Jack made her feel—happy. Like she was enough.

# CHAPTER 4

$\mathcal{I}$t was hard to believe that her time in Linden Falls was drawing to an end. When she and Sophie had arrived, it felt like time stretched ahead of her and went slowly. Twelve weeks was a life-time. Verity was reminded of what it had felt like at the beginning of the summer holidays when she was at school and a six-week summer break from school was an eternity. Then just like that, in the blink of an eye, it was September, and her mum was ironing new blouses, her gym shoes were being labelled, and she was eager to get back into the classroom and see her friends. This was similar, albeit it without the same eagerness to get back to class. Suddenly and without warning, a reminder had popped up on her phone about her return flight to London in a couple of weeks and her heart had flickered. Without fully reading the text, she deleted it and put it to the back of her mind. It felt easier not to think about, not to plan for and not to imagine what it would feel like saying goodbye to Jack and the place and people she had grown so fond of.

She and Jack had fallen into a routine that was easy, comfortable, meeting most days either for coffee on the porch, a spot of fishing, lunch in town, or a nightcap on the deck. Their conversation was always fresh with so much still to learn about the other. In truth, the hours she spent by his side were the most cherished in her day. The pace of their friendship was unhurried, without the frenzied passion she and Sonny had shared when they first met, which, upon reflection, she could see was always on a timer and impossible to sustain. Even Sophie had commented how nice it was to hear her mum laughing so loudly. Verity wasn't sure she could say the same about her daughter, who seemed to spend a lot of time in earnest conversation with Roland, who had a tendency toward the serious. That said, she was entirely grateful that he and Sophie had struck up such a friendship, and one that gave her daughter a different perspective on life. He was the perfect companion to distract her from thoughts of Darius.

It was a big day for Verity, as tonight she was hosting a guest spot at Bistro Claudine. Cassie had been very persuasive.

'So, am I chopping or slicing? I'm nervous of messing it up. I know what you're like in the kitchen.' Sophie held the knife aloft and looked at her with an expression of abject fear.

'Chopping! Finely, tiny little chunks of shallot that

need to all be the same size. It's important, as it's for my tartare.'

'Mum, I don't want to get it wrong!'

'You can't get it wrong, Soph. Whatever you do will be perfect. No one is judging tonight, my professional reputation is not on the line, and I am very grateful for your help.' She saw her daughter's shoulders relax a little. It seemed Verity had successfully hidden the fact that even the *thought* of a misshaped morsel in her tartare made her gut fold with dread.

The invited guests were arriving at seven thirty, giving them just three hours to do the mise en place that would ensure a smooth service. It was the only method she knew. She had roped Sophie in to help with the preparation, and Roland was at that very moment polishing glasses and setting the tables to her exacting standards. In the last hour, she had checked on the placement of jam jars filled with wildflowers and greenery she had foraged from the fields of White Cedar Farm, and each jar was crowned with a single pale rose, courtesy of Phil at Bertie's Petals. The effect was pretty. Her stomach fluttered with the good kind of nerves that were life-affirming. This was to be the first time Jack tasted her food, and she so badly wanted him to like it.

'So is Mr Darby coming for supper tonight?' Sophie read her thoughts.

'Yes!' She pulled a face. 'Bit nervous, actually.'

'You like him, don't you?' her daughter asked as she

delicately peeled the banana shallots, which were fiddly.

'A bit.' She lifted the beautiful whole salmon and scraped at the scales with a fileting knife, keen to put distance between herself and the topic, using the big, fresh fish as a prop.

'You can tell me, Mum. I'm not a kid.'

*You are to me...* 'There's not much to tell.' She danced to the counter, avoiding eye contact with her whip-smart girl. 'Do I like him? Yes, yes, I do. Is there any point in getting overly involved because I am hotfooting it back to Chelsea in a matter of weeks? No, no point at all and so that's that!' She lay the salmon on the chopping block and washed her hands.

'But does it have to be that way? I think it's a real shame that you've met someone who makes you so happy, like Freya does Dad. It feels like such a waste.'

'It's life, Soph. And there's not a whole lot I can do about it.' It didn't grate any less to hear the name Freya trotted out alongside Sonny's; not that she was envious, not now, it was more that it reminded her of the hurt and a situation she was soon going to have to face.

'Couldn't he come to London?'

Verity snorted her laughter at the idea, 'Jack hates going out of Vermont! He only goes to New York when it's absolutely unavoidable, says cities make him itch. He's hardly going to up sticks and bring his fishing rod and easel to our narrow, cobbled streets, is he?'

'I guess not. But as I say, it's a shame. I like him, Mum.'

*I like him too, more than I dare say...*

'I believe the people we meet and the experiences we have are never wasted, Soph, and Jack has taught me a lot, and he's made our trip fantastic. I will forever be grateful to him, Leo, Margot, Paige, Neva, Cassie. Everyone who has shown us such kindness, such love, but'—she paused and considered her words—'our lives aren't here. This is a holiday. We're Londoners. I can't run away from the business or the press or your dad and Freya. I need to buckle up and get on with it, and being here for this magical summer has recharged my batteries and given me the strength to do just that. I shan't ever forget it, not one second.' She chose not to divulge that the thought of leaving Jack layered another spoonful of grief onto a heart that was already struggling.

'Me too. I won't forget any of it.' Sophie paused from the task in hand. 'I've... I've decided, Mum... I've decided I want to kiss Roland and I think I'm going to do it tonight.' Sophie spoke with an uncharacteristic air of nerves.

Verity span around to face her girl. 'Oh.' She dug deep to find the right words and tone. 'I think... What do I think?' She spoke her thoughts aloud. 'I didn't realise you two were friends in that way. I thought you were mates more than possible boyfriend, girlfriend...' She let the idea trail.

'We were, we *are*, but I feel things for him, Mum. I've never met anyone like him.'

'Well, in that case, I think you're mature and smart

and you know your own mind. I also think seventeen is young, even though you might not feel it, and it's an age that plays a kind of trick on you. It fills you with hormones and desires and wants, and yet at seventeen I think you're still a little too young to handle it all. I guess what I'm saying is—'

'Mum,' Sophie interrupted her, 'you know I'm not talking about sex, right? Or anything close to it. I just want to kiss him! Just one kiss, maybe two. I've wanted to kiss him since I met him and tonight's the night. We're going to the lake for a late-night swim after we finish up here and I think I'll do it then.'

Verity stared at her beautiful girl, who was in that twilight zone between child and woman, a girl who knew her mind and whom Verity was so proud of.

'I think Roland is very lucky if he's the person you have chosen to kiss. And thank you for sharing it with me. *I* feel very lucky that you can talk to me like this. I do love you.'

The door from the bistro opened and Roland stood with a glass in his hand. 'Sorry to interrupt, Mrs Joseph, but this one's cloudy. Should I swap it?'

'Yes, thank you, Roland.' She smiled at the tall boy who looked to be all arms and legs, having not yet grown into the man shape he would carry for life. A tall, gangly boy her daughter wanted to kiss.

Cassie bustled in with armfuls of goodies.

'Right, couldn't get hold of courgettes so I picked up zucchini. Will they do? And sadly, no aubergine to be found anywhere, so I grabbed some eggplant.' She dumped the bunch of shiny vegetables on the countertop.

'Very funny!' Verity smiled to stop the wave of melancholy filling her up. It was getting harder and harder not to think about leaving, and Sophie was right —it was a real shame.

Three hours passed in a flash, and before she knew it, the hum of conversation, the tinkle of bottlenecks against the rim of glasses, and the trill of polite laughter filtered back to the kitchen.

'Full house!' Cassie poked her head in the door, and from where she stood, Verity peeked into the bistro, taking in the softly lit interior, the candle on each table, which made the glassware sparkle and the jam jars of flowers that kept things casual yet stunning. It sure was a full house. Neighbours and new acquaintances had all come to support her, and just the sight of them warmed her heart. Even Pam Olson and Steve Turner had turned out. She winced at the amount of butter the personal trainers were about to consume but figured the taste would distract them. Her eyes were drawn to Jack. *There you are...* He stood out to her among the silhouette of strangers. Sitting on a table for three with Leo and Walt, his hair was neat, and his white shirt showed off his tan. He looked good, really good, and not for the first time, she felt the strong flare of physical attraction in her gut. Suddenly he threw his head back and laughed at something Walt had said. She couldn't help but picture the quiet, standoffish man she had met when she first arrived in Linden Falls.

'All set?' Cassie raised her shoulders and rubbed her hands, as excited as she was to get the service underway.

'Let's do this!' She clapped. It was an odd sensation working in a kitchen that wasn't her own and without Dax, Sonny, and the rest of the brigade in attendance, but also thrilling. Here she was, managing alone and in ultimate control of all the food that left the kitchen. It was a huge responsibility, an honour, and the most rewarding thing she had done for the longest time. No one was deferring to or calling for Sonny or sending notes of congratulation via the maître d' to the maestro in the kitchen. It was simply her, a headful of knowledge, a couple of burners, a pan, a variety of seasonings, and one hell of a mountain of fresh and fabulous ingredients.

'Good luck, Mum!'

'Thank you, darling.'

She had forgotten the buzz of a busy service and how quickly the hours passed. The steak tartare topped with a confit egg yolk and served with a sourdough and linseed cracker was greeted with approval. The plates came back clean, and she was happy.

'I think they liked my shallots!' Sophie noted with pride.

'They really did.'

Next, her fish course. She lay the delicately sliced fillets of coral-pink salmon, cured in her own mix of gin, smoked salt, sugar, lemon, dill, peppercorns, and the zest of lime and served them with a spoonful of whipped wasabi mayonnaise and a crunchy shaved fennel salad on the side. The appreciation for the delicate zingy flavour was audible, people smacking their lips together and raving about the taste and texture. This made her so happy! It was more than reward for all her efforts. She took her time with the main course, knowing that the diners' desire for food would not now be based on hunger, not after two courses, but more on the promise of delicious food and the heady smells wafting from the kitchen. Having learned that the trick to good meat was a decent char or crust and the optimum resting time, she gently squeezed the rump of lamb that had lain resting in foil. It was perfect, just the right amount of spring. With the tender slices of lamb, she served her moreish parsnip purée, rosemary-and-garlic-crusted Parmentier potatoes, and sticky honey-glazed carrots, all drizzled with a rich lamb and port jus. Hearty bowls of aubergine, tomato, and courgette gratin with a crunchy topping of bread crumbs and cheese were placed on each table.

'Save me a plate!' Cassie asked as she and Sophie whisked the hot dishes out to the front of house, this the *very* best compliment of all.

Pudding was a traditional crème brûlée with burnt caramel sauce and a rocher of clotted cream forming a delightful puddle as it melted. And after a standing ovation from her appreciative diners and more compliments than she had had in a lifetime, she served coffee and one-bite, handmade, praline-filled chocolates. Jack stared at her, and he looked... proud. It felt nice.

Sophie had rushed off with Roland, flinging her apron the moment service had finished, keen to get to the lake. In the rush and intensity of the evening Verity had all but forgotten that this was the night of the big kiss. She silently wished her daughter well and admired her bravery. It was a great indicator of Sophie's character that she knew what she wanted and was heading off to get it. Now, she sat down at the counter and drank a cup of coffee herself before popping two of the tasty petit fours into her mouth. Her feet and calves had forgotten the ache she was left with after a night of rushing around in a hot kitchen, but with adrenaline coursing through her veins and wearing a cloak of joy at how well her food had been received, fatigue was not a consideration.

The team washed dishes, cleaned the surfaces, scrubbed pans, and wiped down the tables all with exuberance, while Cassie sorted the trash and mopped the kitchen floor. Verity felt like she walked on air, as she stepped out into the town square where the day's warmth had given way to a temperate breeze, which was as refreshing as it was welcome. Jack was waiting for her, leaning on his truck. The Wishing Tree was behind him with the twinkle lights providing star-like brilliance to the moment.

'I don't know about you but I'm starving!' he called. It felt like the most natural thing in the world to run to him, where she fell straight into his arms.

'Get a room!' Paige called from the upstairs window

of her home before laughing and closing the window and curtains.

'Busted.' Jack closed his eyes.

'I don't care who sees us.' She took his other hand and placed it in the small of her back. 'Tonight, I feel like I could take on the world!' Leaning back, she stepped to the side as the two began to dance. And there they smooched and waltzed on the grass, in the centre of the town that had taken her into its heart and made her one of its own.

Jack came to a standstill and pulled her close, and as she stood wrapped in his arms, she could have sworn he was mouthing something, praying maybe?

'Are you... are you making a wish there, Mr Darby?'

'Nope.' He shook his head and led her to his truck. 'Are you going my way? I can give you a lift home.'

'That'd be great.' She linked her arm through his as they ambled across the grass.

'You should have heard what everyone was saying about your food. It was so good!' He held her eye line as they navigated the winding road.

'I really enjoyed doing it. I'd forgotten the buzz of what it felt like and it was so great to have Sophie helping and to have you there. It made it special.' Reaching out, she rested her hand on his thigh.

'The place looked amazing, the jam jars and all those little touches real fancy.'

She was delighted he had noticed. 'I like nothing more than wildflowers. They're my favourite. So delicate and fragile and their beauty fleeting. I value them more than any expensive bouquet.'

'I was thinking'—he let a smile twitch on his lips—'how about I cook you dinner at the weekend?'

'Oh no, not tuna sandwiches!'

'No, not tuna sandwiches and nothing as complicated as we ate tonight, but maybe a decent steak, a good salad, some homemade bread.'

'Ooh, get you! That sounds wonderful. Homemade bread?'

'If Leo can manage that.' He chuckled. 'I might even put on a jacket, go the whole hog.'

'I shall look forward to it. I really will.' She meant it. 'It'll be a special occasion.' She cursed the catch in her throat. The atmosphere suddenly carried weight and the topic was inevitable.

'How do I say goodbye to you, Verty? How do I do that when these are the amazing moments we spend together, and I know I might never see you again? How?'

'I honestly don't know.' She closed her eyes and felt the glossy thrill of her successful night tarnish at the prospect of going home... *home...* 'I honestly don't know, Jack.'

'Me either.' He put his foot on the gas, and they drove the rest of the way with an uncomfortable quiet pawing at them.

He pulled up outside her cabin, and as his headlights scanned the porch, they picked up a figure sitting on the step with her head in her hands. Sophie! And she had clearly been crying.

'Oh my God! Jack!' Yanking at the seat belt, she couldn't get out of the truck quick enough, keen to find out why her daughter sat alone in the dark with tears streaking her face.

'Sophie! Oh, Sophie!' With her heart pounding and fear coursing in her veins, she ran, slamming the door of the truck behind her. 'What happened? Are you all right?' She fell down beside her and gathered her child into her arms, hardly daring to breathe. 'What happened, darling?' she asked more softly now, trying to reach a state of calm while her heart clattered. *If Roland has hurt her...*

'Is there anything I can do, Sophie?' Jack asked softly, as he crouched a little way off, like he knew she might need space, but wanting her to know she was supported.

Sophie shook her head and smiled at him briefly through her tears. 'There's nothing you can do. Nothing anyone can do,' she whispered before the next bout of tears.

'You want me to head off?' he asked gently, again understanding this might be a time for privacy.

And again, Sophie shook her head. 'No, you don't have to go. Shall we go inside?'

'Sure.' Verity helped her stand and placed her arm across Sophie's narrow shoulders. She looked back in anguish at Jack, who returned her gaze with equal concern.

Clicking on the lamp, she guided her daughter to the sofa, where she sat. Verity took the other end and Jack sat in the chair opposite.

'What has made you so upset?' she coaxed her daughter. 'Are you hurt? Take your time.'

'I'm not hurt.' Verity felt the sweet tide of relief, as her daughter continued. 'We got to the lake, and it was lovely,' Sophie began, speaking quickly, as if she wanted to get the words out.

Verity felt her heart race, willing her daughter to speak quickly so she could decide how to react and what needed to be done.

'I... I told Roland that I wanted to kiss him.' Sophie paused.

'Did he do something to you? Has he... Did he...' Verity couldn't help the questions that had been cued up on her tongue as her blood ran a little cold.

'No, Mum! Of course not!' Sophie picked at an invisible thread on her jeans. 'We were sitting in the car looking out over the view and it was so beautiful. The moon was in the water, and I felt like I could jump right into the middle of it. I told Roland I thought I might have feelings for him, feelings that were more than friendship and'—the air crackled with anticipation—'he told me that he loved me, actually loved me, but only as a "no matter what" friend, because... because he's gay. He's gay, Mum, and I didn't know, and I feel so stupid.' She closed her eyes and again her tears fell.

Verity breathed out slowly, aware then that she had

been holding her breath, ashamed that she had feared the worst. 'Oh, Soph.' Her heart flexed for the tender boy. 'That can't have been easy for Roland. And how wonderful that he loves you! That you are his "no matter what" friend! That's really something.'

'It sure is,' Jack chimed.

'Darius wasn't interested in me and now Roland...' She kept her gaze low.

'You are only seventeen, Soph. You have a whole lifetime to figure this stuff out and a whole lifetime for the right person to come along. You'll see.'

'I guess so.' She sniffed. 'Can I get some hot chocolate?' Her daughter wiped her nose on her sleeve, as she and Jack laughed, hot chocolate apparently the cure to all ills.

'I think I'll head off. Seems like you two have a lot to talk about.'

'Jack'—she followed him to the front porch—'thank you for tonight for all your help, support, and for the dance.'

'Think she'll be okay?' His concern was touching.

'Yes, she'll be fine. A hot chocolate, a good old cry, a sound sleep, and tomorrow is another day!'

He studied her face and the look in his eyes was hard to fathom. 'It's not only you and Sophie who need to talk. You and I, we need to—'

'Yes.' She nodded, cutting him short. 'We do. When were you thinking of cooking me that steak?' Reaching out, she ran her hand down his arm and, not for the first time, wished he didn't have to leave.

'I'm dropping some paintings off tomorrow in Burlington, an early start for me, so how about Saturday?'

'That sounds great.' The bubble of excitement rose in her stomach.

'Good night.' He pulled her close to him, and she rested her head in the space beneath his chin where it fit perfectly.

'Good night, Jack.'

She watched his truck disappear down the track and looked up at the sky and the big old moon that Sophie had nearly jumped in. 'How *do* we say goodbye, Jack Darby? You're right, how do we do that?'

*V*erity stood beneath the cascading shower, letting the warm water soothe her tired limbs. She had hiked back to the cabin from Linden Falls earlier, after she and Sophie had got a lift in with Leo. Sophie had gone in to meet Roland, and it had warmed her heart to see the pair hugging as they settled down on the grass in the town square, with coffee and fresh doughnuts from the Cobblestone Bakery. They had a lot to talk about. Roland had waved to her from a distance, and she beamed at him, the gorgeous, smart boy who loved Sophie. He had dropped her home, and they had arrived not long after she had but were a lot less exhausted.

Her shoulders stung a little from exposure to the sun and her calves felt tight. But there was nothing, absolutely nothing that could dull her excitement for the night ahead. Taking her time, she wanted to look her best. Jack was cooking her promised steak supper and had apparently asked Leo if he could borrow a tablecloth and some fancy glasses. Not that she was supposed to know that. He had even called the day before and arranged to come and walk her down the pitted track to his cabin. Sophie had been roped in to assist and earlier in the day had been busy with a reel of fairy lights and the odd candle or two. It was exciting. A night with so much preparation involved couldn't fail to move her, but the event was, she knew, going to be tinged with sadness at the fact that she and Sophie would soon be leaving.

She had started to catalogue every small thing about him, storing it away in her memory for when he was over three thousand miles away. It was a thought too harsh to consider, the looming absence of him almost too much to bear. She was, however, determined not to let their impending separation affect their evening, nor allow her sadness to dilute one second of happiness that was still hers to harvest. Throwing her head back, she let the lather of the sandalwood-scented soap fall over her shoulders and back. With her thoughts wandering, she gulped with a thumping sense of panic.

'Soph, what's the time?' she called out, as she clambered from the shower and grabbed the cotton towel that hung on the back of the door, tucking it around herself in a dress.

'Ten to six!'

'Oh, thank God! I don't want to be late!' She sat down on the small rickety chair by the sink and let her heartbeat steady. Jack was due at seven, plenty of time. 'What are you and Roland up to tonight?'

Sophie had arranged for him to come back over and keep her company.

'Scrabble. And pizza.'

'Scrabble?' she mimed and stifled her laughter, remembering the time she had been concerned that the boy might be a silver-tongued seducer... She wished it were possible to wrap Roland up and take him back to London too. Not only was he the greatest influence on Sophie but also a lovely friend. 'Are you any good at Scrabble?'

'We're about to find out!' was her daughter's joyful reply.

Verity took her time, applying a little mascara and dusting her cheekbones and décolletage with a bronzer. Her scent she sprayed liberally, subconsciously thinking of all the things she could do to help imprint on his memory, wanting, no matter how hard, for him to miss her how she was going to miss him. She fastened the buckles of her strappy heels that had not seen the light of day since they had arrived in the bottom of her suitcase and let the green satin slip dress fall over her head. It clung to her body in all the right places, and she liked the feel of it against her skin, hoping Jack would too. Her hair she left to dry naturally, tousling the layers and roots with her fingers. There was a knock at the door. A quick glance at the clock told her he was a little early, but that was fine.

'I'm off, Soph! See you later, and if you guys need

anything, we are only along the track. And remember to use the board wisely, those double and triple word scores can really—' She opened the door and her heart leapt into her throat. Her intake of breath was sharp and almost cut her, leaving her unable to make a sound. Her hand shook as she reached for the doorframe and her head swam.

'Verity...'

She looked behind him on the deck, wondering if Freya Walsh might be by his side or hiding just out of sight, but no. He was alone. Alone and right here, wearing smart trousers and a crumpled linen shirt. *Sonny...*

'You are so beautiful!' He looked her up and down and she noted the flicker of want in his eyes, something she hadn't seen or felt from him in the longest time. Only a few short months ago, this fact would have filled her with delight, but right now? She felt conflicted. More than a little irritated almost by his presence.

'What are you doing here?' she managed, as he stepped inside her sanctuary, making her two worlds uncomfortably collide. It was surreal and felt invasive. *Sonny was in her cabin! He was here! Here in Linden Falls! But wasn't this precisely what she had wished for?*

'Is that the welcome I get? I've travelled across oceans to find you and that's it?' His tone was jovial, but she could read the truth behind it. He wasn't used to such a downbeat greeting.

'Daddy!' Sophie abandoned the setting up of the

Scrabble board and ran into his arms. Sonny lifted her high and held her close, kissing her forehead as he cradled her to him. 'I missed you!'

'Not as much as I missed you, both of you.' This he addressed to her.

'We've had so much fun!' Sophie wittered, 'I have a new best friend called Roland, who's coming over any second, and you will love him. He's super smart and is going to make robots for a living!'

'Wow, he sounds amazing.' Sonny kissed her again and turned to face Verity, who had shrunk back against the countertop, aware now that the clock was ticking, Jack was inbound, and yet here she was talking to her husband, who had turned up out of the blue, the fact was still sinking in.

'I can't believe you're here.' She took in his physique. He'd lost a little weight certainly, and his hair was newly styled, a bit trendier than she was used to seeing, but he looked good.

'How did you know where to find us?'

'I put a call out to the Wishing Tree!' Sonny closed his eyes and wiggled his fingers in front of him. 'I wished real hard and a vision came to me of where you were… your exact location, in fact.' He put his hands on his hips and laughed loudly. 'What do you think? I asked Soph where you were and she texted me the address.'

She managed a half smile. He had obviously done his homework, read up on the folklore, enough to make her question just for a second.

'You, on the other hand, haven't responded to my texts or emails, so this felt like the surest way to speak to you.'

'I try not to look at emails, a proper detox.' This was true in part, plus she had no desire to see the pictures of Sonny and Freya that would inevitably slip into her feed or read the messages from the wider family, all well-meaning but providing her with a running commentary or their views on '*the pig!*' It was not only unpleasant but a reminder of what she was trying to avoid. 'And the phone signal is pretty nonexistent up here.' This was the truth.

He gave a small laugh and shook his head as if he didn't believe any of it.

'Who's running the restaurant?' She might not have been on hand for the last ten weeks, but knew that with Sonny at the pass, things would run like clock-work, but if Sonny was here...

'Dax has taken on an extra pair of hands in the kitchen, and we're fully booked, reviews are great, all good.'

She nodded. That *was* good. No matter what was happening between them, the restaurant was still their baby, and she wanted to know it was in safe hands. They had put too much into it for it to fail. Folding her arms, she leaned against the wall and waited for him to speak.

'No offer of a drink after my long journey?' He took a step toward her, as if he might reach for her. She took a step to the side, edging closer to the front porch.

'Why have you come all this way, Sonny? What is it you need to say?' She wondered if he were going to ask for a divorce and half admired him doing so in person, deciding in that moment that it was actually the least she deserved after two decades of marriage, although why the hurry, she couldn't imagine. She was, after all, going to be back in London in a couple of days or so. Unless there was an urgency that had sprung up... Was Freya pregnant? Did they want to marry quickly? Could that be it? She glanced at Sophie, who danced in front of the radio, and hoped it would be a smooth ride for her little girl, that they would make her feel involved... She also pictured the headlines, knowing that her very public dumping for a younger model would be small fry if Sonny were to have a baby with the voluptuous, red-lipped food critic. And how did she feel about getting divorced? *A little sad... a little relieved...* came her honest response.

'I've come all this way to tell you that I love you, Verity. That's what I need to say: I love you and I have made a huge, huge mistake.'

The small snort of laughter that left her nose was uttered as much with nerves as shock. 'Are you kidding me right now?'

'Mum, I'm going to shower quickly. Let Roland in when he gets here. Dad you have to join us for Scrabble and pizza!' She jumped on the spot.

'I would like nothing more, Soph. My baby girl.' He wiped the tears that sprung with the back of his hand. 'I'm sorry,' he mouthed as their daughter bounded over and wrapped her arms around his neck in a way that was both forgiving and loving. 'I am so sorry. I shouldn't cry, but I have missed you both more than I can possibly say.'

'You're here now, Daddy.' Sophie planted a kiss on his cheek and headed off to the bathroom.

There was a knock on the doorframe; she turned to see Jack in a neatly ironed shirt and clean jeans. He had brushed his hair and was holding a bunch of wildflowers; the leggy mauve stems lay loosely in his grip. She felt a warm film of nervous sweat over her skin.

'You look...' He paused as a slow smile spread over his face.

'Jack,' she began, not knowing how to start.

'Hello there!' Sonny called loudly, as he stepped out from the shadows inside the cabin, making his presence felt, *the man of the house...* 'Are you here for Scrabble and pizza night too?'

'No, no, I'm...' Jack paused and looked down the track from where he'd just come. The smile slipped from his mouth. 'I'm just a neighbour.'

Verity looked away, not only unable to look Jack in the eye but wary of what might unfold if Sonny knew how she felt about him.

'I... I brought these from Leona, who owns the farm.' He laid them on the porch and took a step backwards. 'You folks enjoy your evening now!' He raised his hand over his head as he walked briskly out into the dusk. It took all of her strength not to chase after him and throw her arms around his neck, to hold him close, to fold into him.

Sonny kicked at the bunch of flowers, scattering them underfoot. 'Don't know who Leona is, but she has terrible taste in flowers. I think she plucked these from a kerbside!' He laughed. Verity felt like her heart might break into two.

'You can't just do this, Sonny.' Leaning on the wall, she unbuckled her shoes and kicked them to one side. 'You can't just pitch up, give a loud apology, and think we will all tumble neatly back to square one. This isn't snakes and ladders, it's our life and you messed it up!'

He took his time in responding, his bravado now replaced with a quiet, earnest note of repentance. 'Where can we talk?' he whispered.

'The deck at the back of my room. It's pretty private. Just give me a minute to get changed.' She closed the bedroom door behind her, an act that was in itself alien when it came to Sonny, the man who had seen her naked more times that she could count and who had held her hand while she gave birth to their daughter. She pictured the food Jack had prepared and the table set with borrowed linen and glassware. *I'm so sorry...* She hoped her thoughts might travel on the breeze and land where he might hear them. Now in her jeans and a pale pink sweatshirt, she opened the bedroom door and took a chair on the deck, trying not to imagine Jack in the same seat her husband now occupied. His presence was still entirely surreal.

'This is some view.'

'It is.' Her tone was a little clipped, no matter how churlish, she didn't want him to have this view. He didn't deserve it.

'I know I messed up—'

'So, what happened, Sonny? Where's Freya?' She cut him short.

He winced. 'It didn't work out. It was never going to and I realised a fraction too late. We had nothing in common, zilch! Nothing to talk about. Turns out great swathes of silence can drive a man mad!'

She thought then of Jack, who found silence to be healing and helped keep madness from his door.

Sonny held up his finger. 'And can I just say that it makes me feel really uncomfortable when you say her name.'

Again, she laughed loudly. 'It does? Gosh, I'm so sorry.' She placed her hand at her throat. 'I don't want to make you uncomfortable. And for your information, it wasn't at *all* uncomfortable for me to have the breakdown of my marriage splashed over the newspapers or to see it on social media, and the fact that you so publicly and quickly took up with Freya Walsh, that wasn't uncomfortable at all!'

'Okay, I get it.' He ran his hand over his face.

'No, you don't get it! You don't get it at all!' She felt her anger bubble to the surface. 'You ditched me, Sonny! After two decades of marriage, you ditched me for something new and shiny and exciting, and you didn't give a shit that it hurt me. You just packed a bag and raced down the stairs as if you had a cab on a meter.'

'I thought it best to just go, like ripping off a Band-Aid—'

'No, you didn't.' Again, she interrupted him. 'Don't pretend you gave me a moment's consideration! You were thinking of yourself, doing whatever it took to make Sonny Joseph happy, just like you always do and always have.'

'That's not fair! I've worked hard for us—'

'Me too!' she cut in. 'I've slogged away for years, but it's not me that gets interviewed or awarded or clapped at the end of bloody service!'

'You *want* to get interviewed?'

'No, but that's not the point! And stop trying to be smart. The point is that I'm not centre stage, not in the business nor in your thoughts, and I don't mind so much about the restaurant, but I always, always thought that when it came to our marriage, our family, we were on the same page. You made a fool out of me, and I deserved better.' She sat tall in the chair.

'You did,' he acknowledged, his eyes misting. 'You did deserve better and that's why I'm here. To show you how sorry I am, to prove to you that it will never, ever happen again.'

'You made your choice, Sonny, and you made it abundantly clear. And now you think you can just turn up here and laugh it off?'

'I haven't just turned up here. I went to great expense and effort to find my way to you, to tell you that I'm sorry, to tell you that I made a mistake and that you are right, I *did* think I wanted something new and shiny and exciting, but I don't, I want you. I want us! I want things to go back to how they were.'

She ran her palms over her thighs and took a deep breath, calming her flustered mind and pulse and feeling a little sorry for Freya Walsh, who had seemingly been dragged into the whole pantomime.

'Is Freya okay?'

'She will be.' He swallowed. 'Can we just rewind? A couple of months, a couple of years?'

'It doesn't quite work like that. You've broken things. You've broken *us* and I don't think we can be put back together in the same shape.' Her bravery gave her confidence that was exhilarating. 'As someone said to me recently, you kind of have to learn to live with the new version of you'—she looked at his face, his expression aghast—'and in all honesty, I didn't *want* things to change, Sonny, but they have and I've had to look at the way we lived. It's given me perspective and I recognise that things weren't perfect.'

'Things are never perfect.' He sat forward in the chair and clasped his hands on his knees in a praying pose, their exchange now calm, almost businesslike.

'That's true, but reflection has allowed me to see that we weren't that happy, not really. We were going through the motions, working too hard, and always chasing sleep or money or moments of joy, distracted by being busy.'

'So, what now?' He stared at her with a look of hope

that only months ago would have made her acquiesce. Instead, she recalled the image of Jack placing the wild-flowers on the porch.

'I don't know, Sonny.' She glanced across the way to the top of Jack's cabin, and her heart lurched in her chest. 'I just don't know.'

'I know I messed up, Verity. Call it a moment of madness. I was flattered, intrigued, but it was hollow, and all I could think about was my girls out here without me and it killed me! Let's not make a plan, let's not give ourselves a timescale, but let's go home and try and work things out. We can't give up on twenty years of marriage, our business, all that we have built together.'

'You did.' She stared at him, her tone and nerve steady.

'And so, take it from one who knows, it was a mistake.'

'So, you've said...' She shook her head at his reasoning that felt thin.

Sophie appeared on the deck. 'Are we on the same flight home, Dad?'

'We are darling.' He coughed to clear any lingering emotion from his throat.

'Yes!' Her daughter did a little dance. 'Mum was a boring flying companion. She watched a movie and snored for hours.'

'Sounds about right.' He looked at her warily, as if unsure of the convention on joking at this point.

'Anyway, I came to say that Roland's here and we're

about to start Scrabble if you want to join us?' Sophie swung on the doorframe.

'I'd love to.' Sonny stood and smoothed his shirt. 'Are you coming?' He held out his hand, and in front of their daughter, she felt obligated to take it. It felt strange, unfamiliar, and quite unlike it used to, where slipping her hand into his was second nature. She walked slowly behind him into the cabin, where a family night of board games awaited. Her stomach jumped at the prospect. She wanted to see Jack, *needed* to see Jack!

'Oh, Mum, don't you have to go and see Mrs Mills first and explain why you can't make coffee with her tonight?' Sophie held her eye line, and Verity felt such love for her child and ally, who was giving her this window.

'I guess I should. Start the first game without me and I'll be back for the second.' She smiled gratefully at her daughter. They exchanged a knowing look, woman-to-woman.

'And don't worry'—Sophie put her arm around Sonny's shoulders—'I'll look after Dad. He needs to try a Twinkie.'

'Don't think I like the sound of a Twinkie!' Sonny protested. 'What is it? Does it hurt?'

Verity splashed her face with cold water and slipped on her sneakers. Running, she couldn't wait to apologise to Jack, to explain what had happened and that she'd had no clue Sonny was inbound. His cabin door was shut, and so she knocked, only realising then that his truck was nowhere to be seen.

'Jack…' She looked left to right, as if she might find a clue to where he could be. It was as she pondered the options that Leo ambled down the track.

'Leo!' She raced over to her. 'Where's Jack?'

'Not eating steak with you, that's for sure.'

'Oh, I know, I know!' She put her fingers in her hair. 'My husband turned up just as I was about to leave. I had no idea he was coming.'

'Is Miss Slinky Knickers with him?'

Despite the dire situation, Verity smiled at the description.

'No, he's alone and apologetic and I don't know what to do! I need to explain to Jack.' Her tone was one of desperation. 'I need to see him!'

'I'm sorry, honey; he's gone up to the mountains. Returned my tablecloth and glasses and told me he'd be out of town for ten days or so.'

'But… but… that can't be right.' The words jammed in her spaghetti of thoughts. 'I'm leaving before then. I won't see him!'

'I think that was probably the plan.' Leo spoke plainly.

'Oh God, what a bloody mess!' Verity closed her eyes and threw her head back briefly. 'Do you believe in the right person, wrong time, Leo?'

'I believe that if it's the right person, it's always the right time, but what do I know?' Leo took a step forward and spoke quietly. 'You've got to follow your heart. That's all you can ever do.'

'I guess.' She sniffed away the tears that threatened and made her way back up the track, walking with a slow reluctance and kicking up dust as the went. The sound of Sophie's laughter bellowed from the cabin, her happy girl. Her daughter was her heart, and she knew she would follow her girl anywhere. And maybe this would be enough...

# CHAPTER 6

*I*t was a ridiculously early start to what Verity knew would be a very long day. She had packed the night before, her actions slow and laboured as with a heavy heart she prepared to go home. With tortured thoughts, robbed of the opportunity to say goodbye to the man who filled her thoughts, sleep had been long in coming.

'You sure you don't want to sit up front?' Sonny asked as he set the sat nav on his phone.

'No, I'm good.' Climbing into the rear seat of the hire car, she knew it was where she wanted to be, hidden in the back. Folded into the corner, she was able to wrap her arms around her body to self-soothe and, with a hollowed out feeling of loss, take one last, lingering look at the place that she was leaving. She also figured she could cry quietly and secretly if she so chose, without having to explain her tears. To her delight and surprise, Sophie took the seat next to her and placed her mother's hand into her own. Verity was comforted by the contact. Sonny jumped into the driver's seat.

'What? Am I the chauffeur now?' he scoffed.

They ignored him.

As the car rolled down the bumpy track, she kept her head down, looking in the opposite direction out over the valley, as the car crawled past Jack's cabin. Awash with sorrow, her tears were thick and salty. She mopped them with a tissue.

The canopy of trees eventually gave way to freeway and with Linden Falls growing smaller in the rearview mirror, she settled back against the seat with rocks of sadness lining her gut. Ironically this was just how she had arrived and for similar reasons—a heart that felt ripped and a spirit that was weighted with loss. She closed her eyes, hoping for the escape of sleep and wishing that, like Dorothy, she could simply click her heels and be home. Her body, it seemed, was exhausted in anticipation of the journey ahead.

Sonny punched the radio into life and an exuberant sports commentary filled the space. It was like another language—*linebacker, quarterback, blitz, handoff, huddle...* She had no idea what was being played, hockey maybe? It certainly wasn't cricket.

'I want to tell you something, Mum,' Sophie whispered.

'What is it, darling?' She cocked her ear to better

hear, expecting it was another revelation concerning sweet Roland, who had cried when the time came to say goodbye.

'I want to tell you what I wished for.' Her daughter twisted in the seat to face her.

'No, no, you don't have to do that... I think sharing a wish means it might not come true.'

'Sometimes yes, but in this case, I think if I *don't* share it, it might not come true. I really want you to see it.'

'Well'—Verity laughed—'two things. First, we know that the Wishing Tree is a load of old baloney, as Jack would say.' Even to say his name out loud caused her pain. 'And second, even if we did have time to go all the way back to Linden Falls, I doubt we'd be able to locate your exact wish. All those branches can look terribly similar. And besides, we've had rain. Neva has probably squirrelled it away,' she joked in a vague attempt to lift her sorrowful heart.

'Honestly, Verity, sometimes.' Sophie sighed as she reached for her phone from the back pocket of her jeans. 'I took a photo of it, duh!' She shook her head as if this was obvious, and not for the first time, Verity felt more than a little "stoopid."

'I'm not sure I want to see it.' She knew that to read her child's words of desire, her innermost hope, no doubt that they would all live as a family again in London just as they always had or that her dad would fall in love with her mum all over again... Well, suffice to say Verity wasn't sure how she should react to such sentiments. Not while her heart still flexed with loss at how she'd missed the chance to say goodbye to Jack.

'Please, Mum. Just look!' She held out the screen, and Verity, with no small measure of reluctance, took it into her hands.

Sophie had chosen a pale blue piece of card, tied with a navy ribbon, and on it her writing was clear and concise. Verity read it once then twice as her heart raced.

I WISH… I WISH MY MUM HAD THE COURAGE TO FOLLOW HER HEART. I WISH SHE WOULD LET HERSELF BE HAPPY…

'All okay in the back there?' Sonny asked from the driver's seat.

They ignored him.

'I don't know what you mean by this…' She read the words again.

Sophie took her time.

'I'm seventeen. I have a couple more terms at school and then I'm off to college. I have it all mapped out.'

'I know, my smart, sweet girl. And I can't wait to see you spread your wings!' She reached out and tucked a loose tendril of her daughter's black, curly hair behind her ear.

'You're always telling me to follow my dreams, do my thing, seek out happiness…'

'That's right. You must. It's what life is all about.'

'But you don't follow the rules yourself!'

'It's different for me. I'm your mum,' she whispered, glad now that Sonny was engrossed in the match. 'I have responsibilities. When you're a parent, you can't really put yourself first.'

'For how long?' Sophie blinked.

'What do you mean for how long?' Verity had lost the thread.

'For how long do you have to do what's best for everyone else? Be there for me? Let Dad come and go as he pleases, humiliate you with Freya Walsh, walk away from the best shot at happiness you've had in decades? How long do you have to keep doing that before you wake up one day and realise that what you say to me applies to you too, and that the best way for me to learn is for you to be my example! You have this *one* life, Mum! This *one* life!'

Lost for words, she took both of her daughter's hands into her own. 'But I like going to sleep and waking up in the same house as you...'

'I like it too, Mum, but in a couple of terms, I'll be sleeping in my college room, and you will be stuck in Chelsea trying to figure out where the time went and wondering what your cowboy is doing at that very minute. And I can tell you that he will be thinking of you, and he will be sad.'

'Oh, Soph!' Now was the time for tears. 'I'm not as brave as you.'

'Not as brave as me? Are you kidding? Who was the woman who stuck her finger on the globe and packed our bags? Who was the woman who started a restaurant when everyone said it was crazy? Who was the woman who didn't fire back, who kept her head when her face was splashed all over the papers?'

'Me.' She felt the rise of something that felt a lot like hope in her chest. 'I did.'

'That's right. And when we first got here, you told me that life pulls the rug from under our feet and you fall so hard it leaves you winded, but that it's all part of the rich tapestry and it makes you resilient, toughens you up. So, aren't you toughened up? Stronger?' Sophie's expression was imploring, before she settled back in the chair and rested her head on her mum's shoulder. Verity kissed the top of her hair, her sweet, smart girl, how she loved her! And how she treasured the weight of her form against her. 'I wish, just for once, you'd listen to me, Mum. I wish you'd take a chance.'

The rest of the journey was spent with Sophie resting in her mother's arms, both wrapped in a blanket of love and connection, a blanket made stronger having spent this glorious summer together, going with the flow...

With the car parked at the airport and the bags unloaded, Sonny popped his sunglasses on the top of his head and reached for the handle of her suitcase.

'That's okay, Sonny.' She took it herself.

'Oh, I forgot, Miss Independent!' He pulled a face at his daughter that in other times would have made her laugh, but not today.

'That's right. I am independent' Her gaze was steady

and her tone calm. 'I'm also not coming back to London.'

He laughed. 'You're joking, right?'

Verity shook her head. 'I've never been more serious about anything.'

'Don't be daft! What do you mean you're not coming back to London? We're at the bloody airport!' He gestured toward the building as if it were not evident.

'Yes, but just because you have arrived somewhere doesn't mean that's where you need to stay. Twenty years of marriage, Sonny. One successful business and one glorious daughter'—she smiled at Sophie—'but you knew you didn't have to stay there. You were happy to walk away. What was it you said? *We are at the end of our path. We need to find new routes and I think we need to navigate them separately.* And you were right. We are and we do.'

'So, what is this? Payback? Revenge? Tit for tat? You've made your point.' He sighed.

Verity shook her head. 'It's none of those things, Sonny. It's time. That's all. It's time.'

'But?' He looked around as if the answer might be found on a billboard or written in the sky.

'But what?' She hitched her handbag over her shoulder and looked at the man who, out of the kitchen and away from the spotlight, actually looked a little ordinary, a little less than.

'But I love you! And what will it do to Sophie? What about the restaurant?' His voice was thin and high.

'I'm fine, Dad. Don't worry about me. I just want Mum to be happy. I want you *both* to be happy!'

Verity stepped forward and kissed her daughter on the forehead. 'I'll Facetime you from the town square and I shall see you at half term.'

Sophie held her tightly. 'I love you, Mummy. I love you so much.'

'Is this some kind of ruddy joke?' Sonny's voice was overly loud, and it bothered her. 'Because it's just not funny!' His voice had gone high, his breathing a little fast. 'What the hell am I supposed to do now?' he yelled.

'You'll figure it out, Sonny. Oh, and if you can't find Wordsworth, try Mrs Roper two doors down. She does like to feed him.'

After one final kiss and a long, lingering hug with her beloved Sophie, Verity hailed a cab.

IT WAS with a growing sense of anticipation in her gut that the taxi wound the familiar path along the ridge. What if she had misread the signals? What if he'd had time to reflect and had a change of heart? What if... Verity closed her eyes and took a breath, quieting the voice of self-sabotage. This was no time for doubt.

'Oh, it's a sharp right ahead. The sign is kind of hidden, easy to miss,' she leaned forward, instructing like a local as the car braked and looped round.

'White Cedar Farm,' the driver read aloud, 'pretty name.'

'Pretty place.' She smiled.

Having paid the taxi driver, and unloaded her bags from the trunk, she walked over the bumpy terrain and up to the middle cabin, where a certain Jack Darby stayed during the summer months. The breath caught in her throat as she spied him. Just like that, there he was loading up the back of his truck with fishing gear. He stopped and did a double take, as if not trusting the sight of her, as she dragged her case behind her, the little wheels getting caught on the rocks and in the ruts.

Abandoning the task, he walked out to meet her.

'You need a hand there?'

'No, thanks!' She waved. 'I got it!'

It was as she got closer that she realized he was smiling, and just to see him again filled her with a heady sense of longing that was intoxicating. She took a step toward him until he was within touching distance.

'Can I help you, ma'am?' he asked slowly.

'Well, I jolly well hope so! I'm wondering if you fancied a roommate?'

He took a slow, deep breath. 'Trouble is I'm not too good with sharing. I find the loud snores of others to be a little disturbing.'

'Oh, don't worry about that. Promise to be as quiet as a church mouse.'

Jack reached out and pulled her into him, kissing her hard and hungrily on the mouth.

She gripped his shirt, never wanting to let go. 'I came back,' she whispered.

'You came back.' He kissed her again.

With her head on his chest, she listened to the slow rhythm of his heart and closed her eyes. It was the sound of home.

'So, what do we do now?' she asked gently, warmed at the prospect of all that lay ahead of them.

'We go fishing!' He took her hand and led her to the truck. She saw he still wore the vintage lure on his belt, and it made her enormously happy.

'Of course we do. We go fishing!'

'I made tuna sandwiches.' He smiled.

'Tuna? I'll never get used to eating tuna in front of the fish!' she pulled a face.

'You gotta let it go, we'll make out it's cheese.'

With her luggage dumped in his cabin and the windows of the truck wound down, Verity let the sun and warm breeze dance over her face before spying Leo foraging for herbs on the track.

'Morning, Leo!' she called.

'Morning!' her friend called back before returning her attention to the hedgerow.

As they drove past the square and the Wishing Tree, Margot came out of the bookstore. 'Hey, Verity!' she called. 'I got that thriller you were interested in!'

'Great, I'll pop by later!'

'Sure!' Margot waved as she disappeared inside the store with Gladys trotting behind.

'Verity!' Cassie called loudly, as she watered the window boxes of Claudine's. 'I need a hand Saturday, busy service. See you about five?'

'Sure!' she waved. 'See you then.' She stared at the handsome man who drove her.

'No one seems surprised to see me.'

'Why would they be? You're where you're meant to be.' He shrugged.

'I think I love you, Jack, and I don't want to be anywhere other than right here.'

'I think I love you.' He solemnly acknowledged this truth. 'And I don't want you to be anywhere other than right here, right by my side.'

'I wish… I wish… I could capture this moment, this feeling! I want to feel like this every day for the rest of my life!' she beamed.

'Careful now'—he glanced at her—'we're in Linden Falls, where wishes have a habit of coming true…'

'But you don't believe in all that, do you, Jack?'

He smiled as the truck headed out of town. 'Me? Believe in all that old baloney? Nope.'

Neva looked out of the window of the Wishing Tree Inn. Long ago she thought if she kept guests coming in and out all through the year, she'd stave off the loneliness that tried to haunt her. And it had worked for a very long time. Despite the fact that she loved everyone in Linden Falls and she knew many of them loved her back, it just wasn't the same as having family.

She sighed.

But this was her lot in life and she had much to be thankful for. Probably more than most, truth be told. And she didn't have time for listless brooding. Happiness was a choice, not a destination, as her mother always told her.

With the creeping despondence now thrown off her shoulders, her face broke into a smile at the sight of Jack Darby's old truck trundling on by with none other than Verity Joseph riding up front. She recalled the day when rain threatened and she had gathered up his wish, cataloguing it in her book, keeping it safe. It had stood out to her, the words so sincere and beautiful.

*I wish she wanted to stay*, it read. *I wish she wanted to stay right here by my side. I think I love her, and I will wish nothing more for all of my days if she might love me back...*

ONE YEAR LATER, *December*

At Jack's insistence they had made the trip into town. Despite an ever-growing to-do list, Christmas fast approaching, and a lurking anxiety for everything to be perfect, Verity had acquiesced and had to admit that the change of pace and scenery was welcome. The cold winter air cut her lungs and sharpened her senses. She walked now with her arm looped through Jack's, as they took in the candlelit porches, bushy outdoor Christmas trees, elaborate front door wreaths, and ornately decorated Wishing Tree. There was no mistaking the holiday season! She inhaled the scent of pine, mulled wine, and cinnamon that wafted from just about every building. It made her mouth water. There was something about Linden Falls at Christmastime that was quite magical.

It felt so very different to how London celebrated. In her home city, the elaborate window displays of Fortnum and Mason, Liberty, and Selfridges were always original and drew enormous crowds who jostled for position, clutching stiff bags embellished with fancy ribbon bows. To see the intricate displays took Verity back to her childhood when she, her sister, and parents would walk from store to store, wrapped up in wool scarves, matching hats, and sturdy boots, marvelling at the fake snow, twinkling lights, animatronic displays of elves and Santa, and piped carols that couldn't fail to put anyone in a Christmas mood. Her favourites were the lights strung across Oxford Street that were, in her opinion, best seen by open-top bus or a convertible, with a thick blanket tucked around her legs. It always felt a little otherworldly to lean back and look up at the dazzle of bright lights strewn across the inky black winter sky of a chilly British December. The reward for all that stargazing would be a pot of hot chocolate and a piping-hot, buttered, toasted teacake cake in the Wolseley on Piccadilly, where chandeliers lit the glass and silverware and the whole interior, with its art deco mirrors and brass and glass surfaces, shone. It was how she imagined life inside a Christmas bauble! The waiting staff stood upright in smart, tailored jackets with silver trays at the ready and a starched white cloth on their arms. Outside would be dark with cars and buses trundling up and down the damp London street, but inside, it felt like time had stopped and she was in a perfect bubble of love with her mummy and daddy and her sister, drinking hot chocolate and feeling the magic of Christmas fill her right up. She could have happily stayed there forever... and had never said as much, but those days, admiring the windows and the taste of that hot chocolate drunk in such opulence had felt far more Christmassy to her than any number of wrapped gifts sitting under a tree. It was one of the reasons she wanted a restaurant, knowing how you could change someone's day, someone's week, someone's life by creating a special moment, a memory, and showing love through the preparing and serving of incredible food.

Jack had laughed when she described the cold London winter. 'The pavement was sometimes frosty, we'd have to take great care not to slip, and we had to wrap our scarves around us to keep toasty. And if you forgot your mittens, you'd know about it! My dad would warm my chilly fingers by holding them inside his, and my cheeks would glow red, leaving me looking like one of Santa's elves...'

'Here in Vermont, it's a little different. Temperatures can plummet to two degrees Fahrenheit. It can even be too cold for snow. Can you imagine that?

'I really can't!'

'Well, it's true. And if you went out without mittens, you could lose a finger to the cold. And when a big snow comes in, the cars get stuck. Walking in it is almost impossible, with snow piled higher than your house! And the sight of a huge snow plough, ready to carve a trench, with headlights blazing, is one of the most beautiful sights you'll ever see. A warm scarf wouldn't cut it either. You need layers, lots of layers, topped off with waterproofs and snowshoes when required.'

Verity smiled at the memory of that chat and tonight, now in her layers and thermal mittens and with her arm looped through Jack's, her thoughts were of London, the city and the people in it who she missed. Alerted by the sound of crying, she looked over to the Wishing Tree where Vera, the beautician knelt in the snow. Huddled forward, she was clearly weeping. It was jarring to see the vivacious woman who was always so sunny, bent and distressed in this way.

'That's not like Vera,' she gasped. 'What should we do, Jack?' her worry hit her like a jolt to the chest.

'We should go check on her.'

It was as they took a step, preparing to cross the square that they spied Neva at the window of the inn. She shook her head, holding their gaze and conveying that she had got this. Whatever was going on with Vera, Neva was keeping watch. Jack raised his hand in acknowledgement and the two carried on their walk.

'What are you thinking? You seem miles away.' He could read her mood.

'I'm hoping Vera is okay or at least that she will be. It's not nice to see anyone upset like that.'

She pulled him to her, mainly for warmth, but also hoping to find a little reassurance. It was going to be hard this year celebrating the festive season without Sophie. Last year she had come to stay when plans to go away with her dad had fallen through. But this year with her beau, Gerry, she was probably right about now sitting on a beach in St. Lucia, no doubt with Grandma Netta in close proximity. Sonny would be planning the evening meal as he snoozed on the sand and listened to the sound of waves lap the shore. Verity envied her daughter a little, not that she wanted to be anywhere other than here with Jack, walking the track where the snow had been swept away, but the idea of the sun warming her chilly bones was something she could get used to.

'I'm also thinking about Sophie.'

'Have you spoken to her?'

'Yeah, but it's not the same. There's something about Christmastime that makes me want to hold her in my arms. I think it's because there's only Sonny and me who remember her early Christmases, and it feels like a time of reflection, and I can't reflect if she isn't here. What am I saying?' She shook her head, speaking quickly.

'What are you saying?' He laughed.

'That I miss her, Jack.' She felt the brush of a mournful mood and shook it off, determined not to let the situation spoil the here and now. This life was, after all, the life she had chosen, and it was a good, good life, one in which she thrived. 'It really is that simple. I *miss* her so very much.'

He pulled her to him and kissed her face. 'I know you do.'

'And I want her to see what we've done with the farm since her last trip!' Her enthusiasm for their home was enough to buoy her spirits.

'She could just look at the state of my hands and my aching back to get a fair idea.' He spoke the truth.

The pair had leapt at the chance to buy White Cedar Farm when Walt's deteriorating health had meant living in a cottage in the centre of town was a far better option. A place where he and Leo could walk for everything they needed. It made more sense. Sonny had generously agreed to buy her half of the restaurant, and with Jack's pictures selling well, they were able to scrape the money to buy the place and at least start the renovations. As to when they would be finished? It was loosely agreed that it would be an ongoing, lifetime kind of project. Jack's old cabin was now his studio and the place he liked to sit and clear his head when old thoughts and troubled dreams came a-knockin'. And on the days when she missed her daughter so badly it felt hard to take a full breath, she would climb up to the mezzanine level of her cabin and sit in the sleeping loft, remembering her child's slumbering form, a jumble of arms and legs on that life-changing summer trip.

'It's getting colder. Shall we head home?' She

smiled, wondering if the novelty of saying that to the man she loved would ever wane.

'Sure, just need to pick up some cranberries. My mom won't conceive of Christmas lunch without homemade cranberry sauce.'

'I'm nervous to cook for your parents,' she confessed.

'You should be!' He laughed. 'Luckily you have a couple of days to practise. They aren't due in just yet.'

Mentally she ran through the checklist of things that needed doing to welcome Mr and Mrs Darby—a display of fresh-cut boughs and berries on the dresser, starched and pressed linen on the beds, a baked ham studded with spices, and a fat pound cake sitting on a wooden board ready for cutting...

Jack steered the truck along the winding lane, and Verity looked out of the window at the branches dripping with snow that sparkled in the winter sun. It was, she thought, as good as any manmade lights strung across a busy street.

He turned sharply onto the track at the sign, which was easy to miss. It was as they climbed to the top of their land, which lay in front of them like a blanket of white, that she spied the flashy navy blue off-roader parked up front.

'Oh no! Jack, please don't tell me that your parents have arrived early! I feel sick. I'm nervous! I'm not prepared!'

He stopped the truck and killed the ignition.

'You are prepared. No one is here to see how good you are at decorating the tree—'

'What's wrong with the tree?' She cut him off. 'I thought it looked okay?'

'Verty'—he took her hands into his, an act that she found instantly calming, a balm of sorts—'you got this. Now let's go inside.'

Cautiously she trod the wide porch, kicking excess snow from her boots and slipping out of them as she shrugged off her waterproof coat and gloves. Now in her thick, knitted socks, jeans, and hoodie, she pushed on the door and felt her knees go a little weak, and her breath caught in her throat at the sight that greeted her. The fire in the den was lit, the tree sparkled, and music played softly in the background. The smell of cooking wafted along the hallway, and there in front of the open fire stood her beloved girl.

'Mummy!'

'Oh! Oh, Soph!' Verity held her breath. Was this real? She had forgotten just how beautiful her daughter was. To see her standing in their home was a glorious, glorious surprise. 'I just can't believe it!' Sophie ran to her. Verity held her tight, inhaling the scent of her and never wanting to let go. 'Sophie, darling! I had no idea! You're supposed to be in St. Lucia!'

'We're heading there in a few days, but I wanted to see you, and Jack said you wanted to see me. It was his idea.'

Verity turned to look at the man who had made this

possible, the man who knew instinctively what she needed.

'Jack.' She felt a swell of affection for her love.

'My parents aren't coming, they're in Boca Raton, but I knew you'd want to get the spare room ready and the house neat. Couldn't think what else to say to throw you off the scent.'

'I just can't believe it!' she repeated, standing back to look at her daughter, who sat somewhere between not looking any different and yet with subtle alterations that meant she was closer to womanhood than child. 'How I've missed you! This is the best, the very best thing!' Her tears pooled.

'Mum, it's so cold! We've built fires. Hope that's okay?'

'Of course, of course, and by "we," you mean Gerry?' She peered around her shoulder, trying to locate the young man she had only met via Facetime, when the signal allowed.

'Ah, no, we broke up.'

'You broke up? Are you sad about that?' She searched Sophie's face for a clue as to her feelings.

'Not really, especially as Roland is coming back to Linden Falls for the holidays and we have big plans!'

'Like what?' She laughed, beyond happy at the enduring friendship between the two.

'Watching reruns of old movies, getting matching tattoos...'

'Great!' Verity smiled, unsure if Sophie was joking. 'So, who did you mean by "we"?' She was curious.

'Verity!' Sonny's voice boomed confidently from the kitchen, as he walked into the hallway that adjoined the den.

'Sonny?' She felt a wave of anxiety at the fact that he was in their home.

'As I live and breathe!' He smiled and raised a hand in acknowledgment to Jack. 'It was Jack's idea, and it's so lovely to be in the snow at Christmas! Like a living snow globe, isn't it, darling?' He turned to talk over his shoulder and from the chintz-covered chair in front of the fire ambled none other than Freya Walsh, the sharp-tongued, red-lipsticked, slinky-knicker wearing food critic.

'Hey, Verity.'

The woman looked sweet, her big eyes a little misty and her manner hesitant, suggesting her sharp tongue and flamboyant nature might be nothing more than a professional mask.

'Freya, welcome.' It was as she looked down that Verity spied the small, rounded belly of pregnancy, which Freya now cradled. 'Oh my! Are you...? Is that...?'

'I am. It is!' Freya sighed. 'A baby boy, who is currently the size of a banana! Although I have to say, I look like a whale and so I think they might mean a whole bunch!'

'I think you look beautiful.' Sonny put his arm around his wife, and Verity noted the very real affection in his expression. He was proud, excited, and rightly so. She was glad he and Freya had managed to iron things out. And she had to admit, her ex seemed a whole lot nicer now that he was no longer her concern. Freya was clearly good for him. Jack closed the front door and stood next to her.

'As a thank you for having us, I am cooking dinner!' Sonny grabbed his wife's hand and they trotted toward the kitchen. 'That was the deal, right, Jack?'

'Yup.' Jack smiled and hung his cap on the newel post.

'So how do you feel, darling, a baby brother?' Verity whispered.

'I think it's great for us all, a little baby!' Sophie cooed. 'We can catch up in a bit, Mum. I'm making the gravy and need to give it a stir.'

Leaving them alone, Verity turned to slip into Jack's arms.

'You really are something, you know?'

'I don't know about that.' He kissed her gently and accepted her hug.

'Thank you, darling, thank you for this wonderful life... I feel like the luckiest woman in the world.'

Freya briefly popped her head out of the kitchen. 'Do you know, Verity, I think Linden Falls is one of the nicest places I've ever been, and your hospitality is the best. I wish... I wish we could stay forever!'

Verity looked up sharply at Jack and felt the colour drain from her face. 'Did she just say what I thought she said?'

He nodded.

'Should we be worried, Jack?'

Jack crossed his fingers behind his back and pecked her on the mouth. 'Nope. Trust me, it's a load of old baloney...'

The End.

# EPILOGUE

*J*ack and Verity are well on their way to their own happily ever after, living a life they love at White Cedar Farm. But what about Neva Cabot? She's made the townspeople of Linden Falls her family for all these years and has been a loyal servant of them and the tree, bringing them gifts of care and objects that she—or even they—don't know they need until she gives them to them. However, when the sun goes down and the big old house gets quiet, she longs for more than only the company of her two mischievous cats, who sometimes seem more like humans than felines.

Secretly, Neva longs for what could have been and what should have been if she had not been short-changed out of her own future. She is humbled and thankful that fate gave her the role of the caretaker of the Wishing Tree, but would she have accepted had she known it was a trade for romantic love? Or for having her own family?

Every night as the stars twinkle through the window and the moon casts a glow of protection over the inn, Neva gives herself just two minutes to think about those sorts of things. Then she closes her eyes and strengthens her resolve to stay positive and continue her important work. She never even considers that the infamous tree might be percolating up a little miracle to send her way.

Not that it'll be easy—Neva will have to do what she's so good at and make the magic come together the way she has for so many others. At least she will if she has any hope of having her own long-ago wish fulfilled. But why would the tree do it now, when it hasn't bothered to do so for all the many decades before? Could this finally be her time? Or is Neva destined to continue watching others have their hearts' desires while hers remains buried deep?

All we really know right now is that Neva will soon have to overcome one of the biggest betrayals of her life in order to help an old friend. She will also be introduced to some new visitors to Linden Falls, and if things unfold in the way that the Wishing Tree would like for them to, Neva's life might just change direction.

TO LEARN MORE about Neva Cabot and the curious happenings at the Wishing Tree Inn, read WISH YOU WERE HERE, the next book in the Wishing Tree series, by Kay Bratt.

⋙

Don't miss any books in the Wishing Tree series:

★ **Don't miss a Wishing Tree book!** ★
Book 1: The Wishing Tree – prologue book
Book 2: I Wish… by Amanda Prowse
Book 3: Wish You Were Here by Kay Bratt
Book 4: Wish Again by Tammy L. Grace
Book 5: Workout Wishes & Valentine Kisses by
Barbara Hinske
Book 6: A Parade of Wishes by Camille Di Maio
Book 7: Careful What You Wish by Ashley Farley
Book 8: Gone Wishing by Jessie Newton
Book 9: Wishful Thinking by Kay Bratt
Book 10: Overdue Wishes by Tammy L. Grace
Book 11: A Whole Heap of Wishes by Amanda Prowse
Book 12: Wishes of Home by Barbara Hinske
Book 13: Wishful Witness by Tonya Kappes

WE ALSO INVITE you to join us in our My Book Friends group on Facebook. It's a great place to chat about all things bookish and learn more about our founding authors.

# ABOUT THE AUTHOR

Amanda Prowse is one of the UK's most prolific storytellers with global sales of over 9 million copies and legions of loyal readers. Born in the east end of London, she is now based on a farm in the West Country. The author of 27 novels and 7 novellas with books sold in 22 countries and translated into over a dozen languages – no mean feat when you consider her first novel was published in 2012! A passionate reader since the age of 6 when a visit to the local library changed her life. Armed with her precious library ticket – she spent hours reading Anna Sewell, Judi Blume and Nina Bawden while scribbling short stories of her own. As a teen, she progressed to authors like Mary Wesley, Colleen McCullough and Maeve Binchy whose gritty, emotional novels would inform her writing. Her mantra is this,

"I want to write the kind of stories I love to read – rich slices of family life packed with characters who are relatable and who, like the rest of us, wade through the sticky pond of life, offering hope and wisdom as they do so and praying they can get to the other side without losing a flip flop."

She is a regular panelist on the daytime TV

programme *The Jeremy Vine Show* on Channel 5 and a popular guest and broadcaster on BBC and independent radio shows. Amanda also narrates her titles as audiobooks. Accolades include winning the Sainsbury's prize for best eBook with *Perfect Daughter*, which was also a World Book Night title of 2016. Her seminal novel *A Mother's Story* was a *Daily Mail* Editor's book of the Year and has also been listed in the Amazon Hall of Fame.

In recognition of being the UK's most prolific writer of commercially successful contemporary women's fiction, Amanda was crowned 'The queen of family fiction' by the *Daily Mail*. Renowned for her emotional novels that place the reader smack bang in the middle of the story, Amanda can be relied on to make readers laugh and cry in equal measure. Always keen to interact with readers, Amanda aims to answer all messages from readers between long and frequent writing sessions and extends a warm welcome for any active readers to join her and fellow founding authors at the My Book Friends Facebook group, where she hosts a fortnightly session on alternative Fridays.

Made in the USA
Columbia, SC
10 March 2022

57492525R00088